A DEVIL

IN PARADISE

THE NEW DIRECTIONS *Bibelots*

KAY BOYLE
THE CRAZY HUNTER

H.D.
KORA AND KA

RONALD FIRBANK
CAPRICE

F. SCOTT FITZGERALD
THE JAZZ AGE

GUSTAVE FLAUBERT
A SIMPLE HEART

THOMAS MERTON
THOUGHTS ON THE EAST

HENRY MILLER
A DEVIL IN PARADISE

YUKIO MISHIMA
PATRIOTISM

OCTAVIO PAZ
A TALE OF TWO GARDENS

EZRA POUND
DIPTYCH ROME-LONDON

WILLIAM SAROYAN
FRESNO STORIES

MURIEL SPARK
THE ABBESS OF CREWE
THE DRIVER'S SEAT

DYLAN THOMAS
EIGHT STORIES

TENNESSEE WILLIAMS
THE ROMAN SPRING OF MRS. STONE

WILLIAM CARLOS WILLIAMS
ASPHODEL, THAT GREENY FLOWER &
OTHER LOVE POEMS

HENRY
MILLER

A DEVIL
IN PARADISE

A NEW DIRECTIONS Bibelot

A complete novel on its own, *A Devil in Paradise* also forms part of Henry Miller's *Big Sur and the Oranges of Hieronymus Bosch.*

Manufactured in the United States of America.
New Directions Books are printed on acid-free paper.
First published as a New Directions Bibelot in 1993.
Published simultaneously in Canada by Penguin Books Canada Limited.

Library of Congress Cataloging-in-Publication Data

Miller, Henry, 1891-1980.
    A devil in paradise / Henry Miller.
        p.   cm.   (The New Directions bibelots)
    Originally published: New York : New American Library, 1956.
    ISBN 0-8112-1244-0 (acid-free paper)
    1. Miller, Henry, 1891-1980—Friends and associates.   2. Authors,
American—20th century—Biography.   3. Moricand, Conrad—Journeys—
California.   4. Occultists—France—Biography.   I. Title.
II. Series.
PS3525.I5454Z463   1993   818´.5209—dc20   93-16389
                                                             CIP

New Directions Books are published for James Laughlin
by New Directions Publishing Corporation,
80 Eighth Avenue, New York, New York 10011

FIFTH PRINTING

A DEVIL

IN PARADISE

Conrad Moricand

Born in Paris, January 17, 1887, at 7:00 or 7:15 P.M.

Died in Paris, August 31, 1954.

It was Anaïs Nin who introduced me to Conrad Moricand. She brought him to my studio in the Villa Seurat one day in the fall of 1936. My first impressions were not altogether favorable. The man seemed somber, didactic, opinionated, self-centered. A fatalistic quality pervaded his whole being.

It was late afternoon when he arrived, and after chatting a while, we went to eat in a little restaurant on the Avenue d'Orléans. The way he surveyed the menu told me at once that he was finicky. Throughout the meal he talked incessantly, without its spoiling his enjoyment of the food. But it was the kind of talk that does not go with food, the kind that makes food indigestible.

There was an odor about him which I could not help but be aware of. It was a mélange of bay rum, wet ashes and *tabac gris*, tinctured with a dash of some elusive, elegant perfume. Later these would resolve themselves into one unmistakable scent—the aroma of death.

I had already been introduced to astrologic circles before meeting Moricand. And in Eduardo Sanchez, a cousin of Anaïs Nin, I had found a man of immense erudition, who, on the advice of his analyst, had taken up astrology therapeutically, so to speak. Eduardo often reminded me of the earthworm, one of God's most useful creatures, it is said. His powers of ingestion and digestion were stupendous. Like the worm, his labors were primarily for the benefit of others, not himself. At the time Eduardo was engrossed in a study of the Pluto-Neptune-Uranus conjunctions. He had delved deep into history, metaphysics and biography in search of material to corroborate his intuitions. And finally he had begun work on the great theme: Apocatastasis.

With Moricand I entered new waters. Moricand was not only an astrologer and a scholar steeped in the hermetic philosophies, but an occultist. In appearance there was something of the mage about him. Rather tall, well built, broad shouldered, heavy and slow in his movements, he might have been taken for a descendant of the American Indian family. He liked to think, he later confided, that there was a connection between the name Moricand and Mohican. In moments of sorrow there was something slightly ludicrous about his expression, as if he were consciously identifying himself with the last of the Mohicans. It was in such moments that his square head with its high cheek bones, his stolidity and impassivity, gave him the look of anguished granite.

Inwardly he was a disturbed being, a man of nerves, caprices and stubborn will. Accustomed to a set routine, he lived the disciplined life of a hermit or ascetic. It was difficult to tell whether he had adapted himself to this mode of life or accepted it against the grain. He never spoke of the kind of life he would have liked to lead. He behaved as one who, already buffeted and battered, had resigned himself to his fate. As one who could assimilate punishment better than good fortune. There was a strong feminine streak in him which was not without charm but which he exploited to his own detriment. He was an incurable dandy living the life of a beggar. And living wholly in the past!

Perhaps the closest description I can give of him at the outset of our acquaintance is that of a Stoic dragging his tomb about with him. Yet he was a man of many sides, as I gradually came to discover. He had a tender skin, was extremely susceptible, particularly to disturbing emanations, and could be as fickle and emotional as a girl of sixteen. Though he was basically not fair-minded, he did his utmost to be fair, to be impartial, to be just. And to be loyal, though by nature I felt that he was essentially treacherous. In fact, it was this undefinable treachery which I was first aware of in him, that I deliberately banished the thought from my mind, replacing it with the vague notion that here was an intelligence which was suspect.

2

What I looked like to him in those early days is a matter of conjecture on my part. He did not know my writings except for a few fragments which had appeared in translation in French revues. He, of course, knew my date of birth and had presented me with my horoscope shortly after I became acquainted with him. (If I am not mistaken, it was he who detected the error in my hour of birth which I had given as midnight instead of noon.)

All our intercourse was in French, in which I was none too fluent. A great pity, because he was not only a born conversationalist but a man who had an ear for language, a man who spoke French like a poet. Above all, a man who loved subtleties and nuances! It was a dual pleasure I enjoyed whenever we came together—the pleasure of receiving instruction (not only in astrology) and the pleasure of listening to a musician, for he used the language much as a musician would his instrument. In addition there was the thrill of listening to personal anecdotes about celebrities whom I knew only through books.

In brief, I was an ideal listener. And for a man who loves to talk, for a monologist especially, what greater pleasure could there be for him than in having an attentive, eager, appreciative listener? I also knew how to put questions. Fruitful questions.

All in all, I must have been a strange animal in his eyes. An expatriate from Brooklyn, a francophile, a vagabond, a writer only at the beginning of his career, naive, enthusiastic, absorbent a˃ a sponge, interested in everything and seemingly rudderless. Such is the image I retain of myself at this period. Above all, I was gregarious. (He was anything but.) And a Capricorn, though not of the same decan. In age we were but a few years apart.

Apparently I was something of a stimulant to him. My native optimism and recklessness complemented his ingrained pessimism and cautiousness. I was frank and outspoken, he judicious and reserved. My tendency was to exfoliate in all directions; he, on the other hand, had narrowed his interests and focused on them with his whole being. He had all the reason and logic of the French, whereas I often contradicted myself and flew off at tangents.

3

What we had in common was the basic nature of the Capricorn. In his *Miroir d'Astrologie*[*] he has summed up succinctly and discriminatingly these common factors to be found in the Capricorn type. Under "*Analogies*" he puts it thus, to give a few fragments:

"Philosophers. Inquisitors. Sorcerers. Hermits. Gravediggers. Beggars.

"Profundity. Solitude. Anguish.

"Chasms. Caverns. Abandoned places."

Here are a few Capricorns of varying types which he gives: "Dante, Michelangelo, Dostoevsky, El Greco, Schopenhauer, Tolstoy, Cézanne, Edgar Allan Poe, Maxim Gorky. . . ."

Let me add a few of the more common qualities they possess, according to Moricand.

"Grave, taciturn, closed. Love solitude, all that is mysterious, are contemplative.

"They are sad and heavy.

"They are born old.

"They see the bad before the good. The weakness in everything leaps immediately to their eyes.

"Penitence, regrets, perpetual remorse.

"Cling to the remembrance of injuries done them.

"Seldom or never laugh; when they do, it is a sardonic laugh.

"Profound but heavy. Burgeon slowly and with difficulty. Obstinate and persevering. Indefatigable workers. Take advantage of everything to amass or progress.

"Insatiable for knowledge. Undertake long-winded projects. Given to the study of complicated and abstract things.

"Live on several levels at once. Can hold several thoughts at one and the same time.

"They illumine only the abysses."

There are the three decans or divisions to each house. For the first decan—I was born the 26th of December—he gives this:

* Paris: Au Sans Pareil, 1928.

4

"Very patient and tenacious. Capable of anything in order to succeed. Arrive by dint of perseverance, but step by step. . . . Tendency to exaggerate the importance of earthly life. Avaricious of self. Constant in their affections and in their hatreds. Have a high opinion of themselves."

I quote these observations for several reasons. The reader will discover, each in his own way, the importance which may or may not be attached to them.

But to get on. . . . When I first met him, Moricand was living—*existing* would be better—in a very modest hotel called the Hotel Modial in the rue Notre Dame de Lorette. He had but recently weathered a great crisis—the loss of his fortune. Completely destitute, and with no ability or concern for practical affairs, he was leading a hand-to-mouth existence. For breakfast he had his coffee and croissants in his room, and often he had the same for dinner too, with no lunch in between.

Anaïs was a godsend. She aided him with modest sums as best she could. But there were others, quite a few indeed, whom she likewise felt compelled to aid. What Moricand never suspected was that, in presenting him to me, Anaïs hoped to unload some of her burden. She did it gently, tactfully, discreetly, as she did all things. But she was definitely finished with him.

Anaïs knew quite well that I was unable to support him, unless morally, but she also knew that I was ingenious and resourceful, that I had all manner of friends and acquaintances, and that if I was sufficiently interested I would probably find a way to help him, at least temporarily.

She was not far wrong in this surmise.

Naturally, from my standpoint, the first and most important thing was to see that the poor devil ate more regularly, and more abundantly. I hadn't the means to guarantee him three meals a day, but I could and did throw a meal into him now and then. Sometimes I invited him out to lunch or dinner; more often I invited him to my quarters where I would cook as bountiful and

5

delicious a meal as he was most of the time, it was small wonder that by the end of the meal he was usually drunk. Drunk not with wine, though he drank copiously, but with food, though his impoverished organism was unable to assimilate in such quantities. The ironic thing was—and how well I understood it!—that by the time he had walked home he was hungry all over again. Poor Moricand! How very, very familiar to me was this ludicrous aspect of his tribulations! Walking on an empty stomach, walking in search of a meal, walking to digest a meal, walking on a full stomach, walking because it is the only recreation one's pocketbook permits, as Balzac discovered when he came to Paris. Walking to lay the ghost. Walking instead of weeping. Walking in the vain and desperate hope of meeting a friendly face. Walking, walking, walking. . . . But why go into it? Let's dismiss it with the label—"ambulatory paranoia."

To be sure, Moricand's tribulations were without number. Like Job, he was afflicted in every way. Altogether devoid of the latter's faith, he nevertheless displayed remarkable fortitude. Perhaps all the more remarkable in that it was without foundation. He did his best to keep face. Rarely did he break down, in my presence at least. When he did, when tears got the better of him, it was more than I could bear. It left me speechless and impotent. It was a special kind of anguish he experienced, the anguish of a man who is incapable of understanding why he of all men should be singled out for punishment. He led me to believe, always indirectly, that never had he done his fellow-man an injury with intent and deliberation. On the contrary, he had always tried to be of help. He liked to believe, and I have no doubt he was sincere, that he harbored no evil thoughts, bore no one any ill will. It is true, for example, that he never spoke ill of the man who was responsible for his comedown in the world. He attributed this misfortune entirely to the fact that he was too trusting. As though it were his own fault and not the fault of the one who had taken advantage of his confidence.

6

Using what little wits I possessed, for I was scarcely more capable than he in practical matters, I finally hit upon the idea of asking my friends to have Moricand do their horoscopes for a modest fee. I believe I suggested a hundred francs as a fee, but it may only have been fifty. One could then get a very decent meal for from twelve to fifteen francs. As for Moricand's room rent, it could not have been more than three hundred francs per month, possibly less.

All went well until I exhausted my list of friends and acquaintances. Then, not to let Moricand down, I began inventing people. That is to say, I would give him the name, sex, date, hour and place of birth of individuals who did not exist. I paid for these horoscopes out of my own pocket, naturally. According to Moricand, who had not the least suspicion of the turn things had taken, these imaginary subjects comprised an astounding variety of characters. Occasionally, faced with a most incongruous chart, he would express a desire to meet the subject, or would press me for intimate details which of course I would offer with the ease and nonchalance of one who knew whereof he spoke.

When it came to reading personalities, Moricand impressed one as possessing certain powers of divination. His sixth sense, as he called it, served him well in interpreting a chart. But often he had no need of a chart, no need of dates, places, and so on. Never shall I forget the banquet given by the group sponsoring the revue *Volontés* which was directed by Georges Pelorson. Eugene Jolas and I were the only Americans in the group, the rest were all French. There must have been about twenty of us at table that evening. The food was excellent and the wine and liqueurs plentiful. Moricand sat opposite me. On one side of him sat Jolas and on the other, I believe, Raymond Queneau. Every one was in excellent spirits, the conversation running high.

With Moricand in our midst, it was inevitable that sooner or later the subject of astrology must come up for discussion. There he was, Moricand, cool as a cucumber, and filling his breadbasket

7

to the best of his ability. Lying in wait, as it were, for the jeers and derision which he doubtless anticipated.

And then it came—an innocent question by an unsuspecting nobody. Immediately a sort of mild insanity pervaded the atmosphere. Questions were being hurled from all directions. It was as if a fanatic had suddenly been uncovered—or worse, a lunatic. Jolas, who was a little under the weather by now and consequently more aggressive than usual, insisted that Moricand give demonstrable proofs. He challenged Moricand to single out the various zodiacal types seated about him. Now Moricand had undoubtedly made such classification in his head during the course of his conversation with this one and that. He could not help doing so by virtue of his calling. It was everyday routine with him, when talking to an individual, to observe the person's manner of speech, his gestures, his tics and idiosyncrasies, his mental and physical build, and so on. He was acute enough, adept enough, to distinguish and classify the more pronounced types present at the table. So, addressing himself to one after another whom he had singled out, he named them: Leo, Taurus, Libra, Virgo, Scorpio, Capricorn, and so on. Then, turning to Jolas, he quietly informed him that he believed he could tell him the year and day of his birth, perhaps the hour too. So saying, he took a good pause, raised his head slightly, as if studying the look of the heavens on the appointed day, then gave the exact date and, after a further pause, the approximate hour. He had hit it right on the nose. Jolas, who was dumbfounded, was still catching his breath as Moricand went on to relate some of the more intimate details of his past, facts which not even Jolas' close friends were aware of. He told him what he liked and what he disliked; he told him what maladies he had suffered from and was likely to suffer from in the future; he told him all manner of things which only a mind-reader could possibly divulge. If I am not mistaken, he even told him the location of a birthmark. (A shot in the dark like this was a trump card that Moricand loved to play when he had things well in hand. It was like putting his signature to a horoscope.)

8

That was one occasion when he ran true to form. There were others, some of them more eerie, more disturbing. Whenever it happened it was a good act. Far better than a spiritualistic séance.

Thinking of these performances, my mind always reverts to the room he occupied on the top floor of his hotel. There was no elevator service, naturally. One had to climb the five or six flights to the attic. Once inside, the world outside was completely forgotten. It was an irregular shaped room, large enough to pace up and down in, and furnished entirely with what belongings Moricand had managed to salvage from the wreck. The first impression one had, on entering, was that of orderliness. Everything was in place, but exactly in place. A few millimeters this way or that in the disposal of a chair, an *objet d'art*, a paper knife, rubbers and the effect would have been lost—in Moricand's mind, at least. Even the arrangement of his writing table revealed this obsession with order. Nowhere at any time was there ever any trace of dust or dirt. All was immaculate.

He was the same about his own person. He always appeared in clean, starched linen, coat and pants pressed (he probably pressed them himself), shoes polished, cravat arranged just so and to match his shirt of course, hat, overcoat, rubbers and suchlike neatly arranged in the clothes closet. One of the most vivid remembrances he had of his experience in the First World War—he had served in the Foreign Legion—was of the filth which he had been obliged to endure. He once recounted to me at great length how he had stripped and washed himself from head to toe with wet snow (in the trenches) after a night in which one of his comrades had vomited all over him. I had the impression that he would far rather have suffered a bullet wound than an ordeal of this nature.

What sticks in my crop about this period, when he was so desperately poor and miserable, is the air of elegance and fastidiousness which clung to him. He always seemed more like a stockbroker weathering a bad period than a man utterly without resources. The clothes he wore, all of excellent cut as well as of the best material, would obviously last another ten years, considering the care and

9

attention he gave them. Even had they been patched, he would still have looked the well-dressed gentleman. Unlike myself, it never occurred to him to pawn or sell his clothes in order to eat. He had need of his good clothes. He had to preserve a front were he to maintain even interrupted relations with *le monde*. Even for ordinary correspondence he employed good stationery. Slightly perfumed too. His handwriting, which was distinctive, was also invested with the traits I have underlined. His letters, like his manuscripts and his astrological portraits, bore the stamp of a royal emissary, of a man who weighed every word carefully and would vouch for his opinions with his life.

One of the objects in this den he inhabited I shall never forget as long as I live. The dresser. Towards the end of an evening, usually a long one, I would edge toward this dresser, wait for a propitious moment when his glance was averted, and deftly slip a fifty- or hundred-franc note under the statuette which stood on top of the dresser. I had to repeat this performance over and over because it would have embarrassed him, to say the least, had I handed him the money or sent it to him in the mail. I always had the feeling, on leaving, that he would give me just time enough to reach the nearest Métro station, then duck out and buy himself a *choucroute garnie* at a nearby *brasserie*.

I must also say that I had to be very careful about expressing a liking for anything he possessed, for if I did he would thrust it on me in the manner of a Spaniard. It made no difference whether I admired a cravat he was wearing or a walking stick, of which he still had a number. It was thus I inadvertently acquired a beautiful cane which Moïse Kisling had once given him. On one occasion it demanded all my powers of persuasion to prevent him from giving me his only pair of gold cuff links. Why he was still wearing starched cuffs and cuff links I never dared ask him. He would probably have answered that he had no other kind of shirts.

On the wall by the window, where he had arranged his writing

10

table caticornered, there were always pinned up two or three charts of subjects whose horoscopes he was studying. He kept them there at his elbow just as a chess player keeps a board handy on which he has a problem arranged. He believed in allowing time for his interpretations to simmer. His own chart hung beside the others in a special niche.

He regarded it at frequent intervals, much as a mariner would a barometer. He was always waiting for an "opening." In a chart, he told me, death manifested itself when all the exits were blocked. It was difficult, he averred, to detect the advent of death in advance. It was much easier to see it after a person had died; then everything became crystal clear, dramatic from a graphic standpoint.

What I recall most vividly are the red and blue pencil marks he employed to indicate the progress or regression of the span of chance in his chart. It was like watching the movement of a pendulum, a slow moving pendulum which only a man of infinite patience would bother to follow. If it swung a little this way, he was almost jubilant; if it swung a little the other way, he was depressed. What he expected of an "opening" I still do not know, since he was never prepared to make any apparent effort to improve his situation. Perhaps he expected no more than a breather. All he could possibly hope for, given his temperament, was a windfall. Certainly nothing in the way of a job could have meant anything to him. His one and only desire was to continue his researches. Seemingly, he had reconciled himself to his limitations. He was not a man of action, not a brilliant writer who might some day hope to liberate himself by the pen, nor was he flexible and yielding enough to beg his way. He was simply Moricand, the personality so clearly revealed by the chart which he himself had drawn up. A "subject" with a bad Saturn, among other things. A sad wizard who in moments of desperation would endeavor to extract a thin ray of promise from his star Regulus. In short, a victim doomed to live a dolorous, circumscribed life.

"We all get a break some time or other," I used to say to him.

11

"It can't rain all the time! And what about that saying—"It's an ill wind that blows no one some good'?"

If he was in a mood to listen I might even go further and say: "Why don't you forget the stars for a while? Why not take a vacation and act *as if* fortune were yours? Who knows what might happen? You might meet a man in the street, an utter stranger, who would be the means of opening these doors you regard as locked. There is such a thing as grace too. It could happen, you know, if you were in the right mood, if you were prepared to let something happen. And if you forgot what was written in the sky."

To a speech of this sort he would give me one of those strange looks which signified many things. He would even throw me a smile, one of those tender, wistful smiles which an indulgent parent gives a child who poses an impossible problem. Nor would he rush to offer the answer which he had ever at his disposal and which, no doubt, he was weary of stating when thus cornered. In the pause which followed he gave the impression that he was first testing his own convictions, that he was rapidly surveying (for the thousandth time) all that he had ever said or thought about the subject, that he was even giving himself an injection of doubt, widening and deepening the problem, giving it dimensions which neither I nor anyone else could imagine, before slowly, ponderously, coldly and logically formulating the opening phrases of his defense.

"*Mon vieux*," I can hear him saying, "One must understand what is meant by chance. The universe operates according to law, and these laws obtain as much for man's destiny as for the birth and movements of the planets." Leaning back in his comfortable swivel chair, veering slightly round to focus better on his chart, he would add: "Look at *that!*" He meant the peculiar and particular impasse in which he was fixed at the moment. Then, extracting my chart from the portfolio which he always kept handy, he would beg me to examine it with him. "The only chance for me at this moment," he would say most solemnly, "is *you*. There *you* are!" And he would indicate how and where I fitted into the picture.

12

"You and that angel, Anaïs. Without you two I would be a goner!"

"But why don't you look at it more positively?" I would exclaim. "If we are there, Anaïs and I, if we are all that you credit us with being, why don't you put all your faith and trust in us? Why don't you let us help you to free yourself? There are no limits to what one person can do for another, is that not so?"

Of course he had an answer to that. His great failing was that he had an answer for everything. He did not deny the power of faith. What he would say quite simply was that he was a man to whom faith had been denied. It was there in his chart, the absence of faith. What could one do? What he failed to add was that he had chosen the path of knowledge, and that in doing so he had clipped his own wings.

Only years later did he offer me a glimpse into the nature and origin of this castration which he referred to as lack of faith. It had to do with his boyhood, with the neglect and indifference of his parents, the perverse cruelty of his schoolmasters, one in particular, who had humiliated and tortured him in inhuman fashion. It was an ugly, woeful story, quite enough to account for his loss of morale, his spiritual degradation.

As always before a war, there was fever in the air. With the end approaching, everything became distorted, magnified, speeded up. The wealthy were as active as bees or ants, redistributing their funds and assets, their mansions, their yachts, their gilt-edged bonds, their mine holdings, their jewels, their art treasures. I had at the time a good friend who was flying back and forth from one continent to another catering to these panicky clients who were trying to get out from under. Fabulous were the tales he told me. Yet so familiar. So disgustingly familiar. (Can anyone imagine an army of millionaires?) Fabulous too were the tales of another friend, a chemical engineer, who would turn up at intervals for dinner, just back from China, Manchuria, Mongolia, Tibet, Persia, Afghanistan, wherever there was deviltry afoot. And always with the same story—of intrigue, plunder, bribery, treachery, plots and projects of

13

the most diabolical sort. The war was still a year or so away, but the signs were unmistakable—not only for the wars and revolutions to follow.

Even the "bohemians" were being routed out of their trenches. Amazing how many young intellectuals were already dislocated, dispossessed, already being pushed about like pawns in the service of their unknown masters. Every day I was receiving visits from the most unexpected individuals. There was only one question in every one's mind: *when?* Meanwhile make the most of it! And we did, we who were hanging on till the last boat call.

In this merry, devil-may-care atmosphere Moricand took no part. He was hardly the sort to invite for a festive evening which promised to end up in a brawl, a drunken stupor, or a visit from the police. Indeed, the thought never entered my head. When I did invite him over for a meal I would carefully select the two or three guests who were to join us. They were usually the same ones each time. Astrological buddies, so to speak.

Once he called on me unannounced, a rare breach of protocol for Moricand. He seemed elated and explained that he had been strolling about the quays all afternoon. Finally he fished a small package out of his coat pocket and handed it to me. "For *you!*" he said, with much emotion in his voice. From the way he said it I understood that he was offering a gift which only I could appreciate to the full.

The book, for that's what it was, was Balzac's *Seraphita.*

Had it not been for *Seraphita* I doubt very much that my adventure with Moricand would have terminated in the manner it did. It will be seen shortly what a price I paid for this precious gift.

What I wish to stress at this point is that, coincident with the feverishness of the times, the increased tempo, the peculiar derangement which everyone suffered, writers more than others perhaps, there was noticeable, in my own case at any rate, a quickening of the spiritual pulse. The individuals who were thrown across my path, the incidents which occurred daily and which to another

14

would have seemed like trifles, all had a very special significance in my mind. There was an *enchainement* which was not only stimulating and exciting but often hallucinating. Just to take a walk into the outskirts of Paris—Montrouge, Gentilly, Kremlin-Bicêtre, Ivry—was sufficient to unbalance me for the rest of the day. I enjoyed being unbalanced, derailed, disoriented early in the morning. (The walks I refer to were "constitutionals," taken before breakfast. My mind free and empty, I was making myself physically and spiritually prepared for long sieges at the machine.) Taking the rue de la Tombe-Issoire, I would head for the outer boulevards, then dive into the outskirts, letting my feet lead me where they would. Coming back, I always steered instinctively for the Place de Rungis, which in some mysterious way connected itself with certain phases of the film *L'Age d'or*, and more particularly with Luis Bunuel himself. With its queer street names, its atmosphere of not belonging, its special assortment of gamins, urchins and monsters who hailed from some other world, it was for me an eerie and seductive neighborhood. Often I took a seat on a public bench, closed my eyes for a few moments to sink below the surface, then suddenly opened them to look at the scene with the vacant stare of a somnambulist. Goats from the *banlieue*, gangplanks, douche bags, safety belts, iron trusses, *passerelles* and *sauterelles* floated before my glazed eyeballs, together with headless fowl, beribboned antlers, rusty sewing machines, dripping ikons and other unbelievable phenomena. It was not a community or neighborhood but a vector, a very special vector created wholly for my artistic benefit, created expressly to tie me into an emotional knot. Walking up the rue de la Fontaine à Mulard, I struggled frantically to contain my ecstasy, struggled to fix and hold in my mind (until after breakfast) three thoroughly disparate images which, if I could fuse them successfully, would enable me to force a wedge into a difficult passage (of my book) which I had been unable to penetrate the day before. The rue Brillat-Savarin, running like a snake past the Place, balances the works of Eliphas Lévi,

15

the rue Butte aux Cailles (farther along) evokes the Stations of the Cross, the rue Félicien Rops (at another angle) sets bells to ringing and with it the whir of pigeon wings. If I was suffering from a hangover, as I frequently was, all these associations, deformations and interpenetrations became even more quixotically vivid and colorful. On such days it was nothing to receive in the first mail a second or third copy of the *I Ching*, an album of Scriabin, a slim volume concerning the life of James Ensor or a treatise on Pico della Mirandola. Beside my desk, as a reminder of recent festivities, the empty wine bottles were always neatly ranged: Nuits Saint-Georges, Gevrey-Chambertin, Clos-Veugeot, Vosne Romanée, Meursault, Traminer, Château Haut-Brion, Chambolle-Musigny, Montrachet, Beaune, Beaujolais, Anjou and that *"vin de prédilection"* of Balzac's—Vouvray. Old friends, even though drained to the last drop. Some still retained a slight bouquet.

Breakfast, *chez moi.* Strong coffee with hot milk, two or three delicious warm croissants with sweet butter and a touch of jam. And with the breakfast a snatch of Segovia. An emperor couldn't do better.

Belching a little, picking my teeth, my fingers tingling, I take a quick look around (as if to see if everything's in order!), lock the door, and plunk myself in front of the machine. Set to go. My brain afire.

But what drawer of my Chinese cabinet mind will I open first? Each one contains a recipe, a prescription, a formula. Some of the items go back to 6,000 B.C. Some still further back.

First I must blow the dust away. Particularly the dust of Paris, so fine, so penetrating, so nearly invisible. I must submerge to the root taps—Williamsburg, Canarsie, Greenpoint, Hoboken, the Gowanus Canal, Erie Basin, to playmates now moldering in the grave, to places of enchantment like Glendale, Glen Island, Sayville, Patchogue, to parks and islands and coves now transformed into garbage dumps. I must think French and write English, be very still and talk wild, act the sage and remain a fool or a dunce. I must balance what is unbalanced without falling off the tightrope. I must summon to the hall of vertigo the lyre known as the Brooklyn Bridge yet preserve the flavor and the aroma of the Place de Rungis. It must be of this moment but pregnant with the ebb of the Great Return. . . .

And it was just at this time—too much to do, too much to see, too much to drink, too much to digest—that, like heralds from distant yet strangely familiar worlds, the books began to come. Nijinsky's *Diary, The Eternal Husband, The Spirit of Zen, The Voice of the Silence, The Absolute Collective,* the *Tibetan Book of the Dead, l' Eubage,* the *Life of Milarepa, War Dance, Musings of a Chinese Mystic. . . .*

Some day, when I acquire a house with a large room and bare walls, I intend to compose a huge chart or graph which will tell better than any book the story of my friends, and another telling the story of the books in my life. One on each wall, facing each other, impregnating each other, erasing each other. No man can hope to live long enough to round out these happenings, these unfathomable experiences, in words. It can only be done symbolically, graphically, as the stars write their constellated *mysterium.*

Why do I speak thus? Because during this period—too much to do, too much to see, taste, and so forth—the past and the future converged with such clarity and precision that not only friends and books but creatures, objects, dreams, historical events, monuments, streets, names of places, walks, encounters, conversations, reveries, half-thoughts, all came sharply into focus, broke into angles, chasms, waves, shadows, revealing to me in one harmonious, understandable pattern their essence and significance.

Where my friends were concerned, I had only to think a moment in order to evoke a company or a regiment. Without effort on my part they ranged themselves in order of magnitude, influence, duration, proximity, spiritual weight and density, and so on. As they took their stations I myself seemed to be moving through the ether with the sweep and rhythm of an absent-minded angel,

17

yet falling in with each in turn at exactly the right zodiacal point and at precisely the destined moment, good or bad, to tune in. What a medley of apparitions they presented! Some were shrouded in fog, some sharp as sentinels, some rigid as phantom ice-bergs, some wilted like autumn flowers, some racing toward death, some rolling along like drunks on rubber wheels, some pushing laboriously through endless mazes, some skating over the heads of their comrades as if muffled in luminol, some lifting crushing weights, some glued to the books in which they burrowed, some trying to fly though anchored with ball and chain, but all of them vivid, named, classified, identified according to need, depth, insight, flavor, aura, fragrance and pulse beat. Some were suspended like blazing planets, others like cold, distant stars. Some burgeoned with frightening rapidity, like novae, then faded into dust; some moved along discreetly, always within calling distance, as it were, like beneficent planets. Some stood apart, not haughtily but as if waiting to be summoned—like authors (Novalis, for example) whose names alone are so freighted with promise that one postpones reading them until that ideal moment which never arrives.

And Moricand, had he any part in all this scintillating turmoil? I doubt it. He was merely part of the décor, another phenomenon pertinent to the epoch. I can see him still as he then appeared in my mind's eye. In a penumbra he lurks, cool, gray, imperturbable, with a twinkle in his eyes and a metallic *"Ouais!"* shaping his lips. As if saying to himself: *"Ouais! Tu parles!"* Know it all. Heard it before. Forgot it long ago. *Ouais! Tu parles!* The labyrinth, the chamois with the golden horns, the grail, the argonaut, the *kermesse à la Breughel*, the wounded groin of Scorpio, the profanation of the host, the Areopagite, translunacy, symbiotic neurosis, and in a wilderness of pebbles a lone katydid. Keep it up, the wheel is softly turning. A time comes when. . . ." Now he is bent over his *pantacles*. Reads with a Geiger counter. Unlatching his gold fountain pen, he writes in purple milk: Porphyry, Proclus, Plotinus, Saint Valentin, Julian the Apostate, Hermes Trismegistus, Apollonius of Tyana, Claude Saint-Martin. In his vest pocket he carries a little phial; it contains myrrh, frankincense and a dash of wild sarsparilla. *The odor of sanctity!* On the little finger of his left hand he wears a jade ring marked with yin and yang. Cautiously he brings out a heavy brass watch, a stem-winder, and lays it on the floor. It is 9:30, sidereal time, the moon on the cusp of panic, the ecliptic freckled with cometary warts. Saturn is there with her ominous milky hue. *"Ouais!"* he exclaims, as if clinching the argument. "I say nothing against anything. I observe. I analyze. I calculate. I distillate. Wisdom is becoming, but knowledge is the certainty of certitude. To the surgeon his scalpel, to the gravedigger his pick and shovel, to the analyst his dream books, to the fool his dunce cap. As for me, I have a bellyache. The atmosphere is too rarefied, the stones too heavy to digest. *Kali Yuga.* Only 9,765,854 years to go and we will be out of the snake pit. *Du courage, mon vieux!"*

Let us take a last look backward. The year is 1939. The month is June. I am not waiting for the Huns to rout me out. I am taking a vacation. Another few hours and I shall be leaving for Greece.

All that remains of my presence in the studio at the Villa Seurat is my natal chart done in chalk on the wall facing the door. It's for whomever takes over to ponder on. I'm sure it will be an officer of the line. Perhaps an erudite.

Oh yes, and on the other wall, high up near the ceiling, these two lines:

Jetzt müsste die Welt versinken,
Jetzt musste ein Wunder gescheh'n.

Clear, what?
And now it is my last evening with my good friend Moricand. A modest repast in a restaurant on the rue Fontaine, diagonally opposite the living quarters of the Father of Surrealism. We spoke

19

of him as we broke bread. *Nadja* once more. And the "Profanation of the Host."

He is sad, Moricand. So am I, in a faint way. I am only partly there. My mind is already reaching out for Rocamadour where I expect to be on the morrow. In the morning Moricand will once again face his chart, observe the sway of the pendulum—undoubtedly it has moved to the left!—see if Regulus, Rigel, Antares or Betelgeuse can aid him just a wee, wee bit. Only 9,765,854 years before the climate changes. . . .

It's drizzling as I step out of the Métro at Vavin. I've decided I must have a drink all by my lonesome. Does not the Capricorn love solitude? *Ouais!* Solitude in the midst of hubbub. Not heavenly solitude. Earthly solitude. *Abandoned places.*

The drizzle turns into a light rain, a gray, sweetly melancholy rain. A beggar's rain. My thoughts drift. Suddenly I'm gazing at the huge chrysanthemums my mother loved to raise in our dismal back yard in the street of early sorrows. They are hanging there before my eyes, like an artificial bloom, just opposite the lilac bush which Mr. Fuchs, the hundski picker, gave us one summer.

Yes, the Capricorn is a beast of solitude. Slow, steady, persevering. Lives on several levels at once. Thinks in circles. Fascinated by death. Ever climbing, climbing. In search of the edelweiss, presumably. Or could it be the *immortelle?* Knows no mother. Only "the mothers." Laughs little and usually on the wrong side of the face. Collects friends as easily as postage stamps, but is unsociable. Speaks truthfully instead of kindly. Metaphysics, abstractions, electromagnetic displays. Dives to the depths. Sees stars, comets, asteroids where others see only moles, warts, pimples. Feeds on himself when tired of playing the man-eating shark. A paranoiac. An *ambulatory* paranoiac. But constant in his affections—*and his hatreds. Ouais!*

From the time the war broke out until 1947 not a word from Moricand. I had given him up for dead. Then, shortly after we had installed ourselves in our new home on Partington Ridge, a thick envelope arrived bearing the return address of an Italian princess. In it was enclosed a letter from Moricand, six months old, which he had requested the princess to forward should she ever discover my address. He gave as his address a village near Vevey, Switzerland, where he said he had been living since the end of the war. I answered immediately, telling him how glad I was to know that he was still alive and inquiring what I could do for him. Like a cannon ball came his reply, giving a detailed account of his circumstances which, as I might have guessed, had not improved. He was living in a miserable pension, in a room without heat, starving as usual, and without even the little it takes to buy cigarettes. Immediately we began sending him foodstuffs and other necessities of which he was apparently deprived. And what money we could spare. I also sent him international postal coupons so that he would not be obliged to waste money on stamps.

Soon the letters began to fly back and forth. With each succeeding letter the situation grew worse. Obviously the little sums we dispatched didn't go very far in Switzerland. His landlady was constantly threatening to turn him out, his health was getting worse, his room was insupportable, he had not enough to eat, it was impossible to find work of any kind, *and*—in Switzerland you don't beg!

To send him larger sums was impossible. We simply didn't have that kind of money. What to do? I pondered the situation over and over. There seemed to be no solution.

Meanwhile his letters poured in, always on good stationery, always airmail, always begging, supplicating, the tone growing more and more desperate. Unless I did something drastic he was done for. That he made painfully clear.

Finally I conceived what I thought to be a brilliant idea. Genial, nothing less. It was to invite him to come and live with us, share what we had, regard our home as his own for the rest of his days. It was such a simple solution I wondered why it had **never oc-**cured to me before.

I kept the idea to myself for a few days before broaching it to

21

my wife. I knew that it would take some persuading to convince her of the necessity for such a move. Not that she was ungenerous, but that he was hardly the type to make life more interesting. It was like inviting Melancholia to come and perch on your shoulder.

"Where would you put him up?" were her first words, when finally I summoned the courage to broach the subject. We had only a living room, in which we slept, and a tiny wing adjoining it where little Val slept.

"I'll give him my studio," I said. This was a separate cubicle hardly bigger than the one Val slept in. Above it was the garage which had been partly converted into a workroom. My thought was to use that for myself.

Then came the big question: "How will you raise the passage money?"

"That I have to think about," I replied. "The main thing is, are you willing to risk it?"

We argued it back and forth for several days. Her mind was full of premonitions and forebodings. She pleaded with me to abandon the idea. "I know you'll only regret it," she croaked. What she could not understand was why I felt it imperative to assume such a responsibility for one who had never really been an intimate friend. "If it were Perlès," she said, "it would be different; he means something to you. Or your Russian friend, Eugene. But Moricand? What do you owe *him?*"

This last touched me off. What did I owe Moricand? Nothing. *And everything.* Who was it put *Seraphita* in my hands? I endeavored to explain the point. Halfway along I gave up. I saw how absurd it was to attempt to make such a point. A mere book! One must be insane to fall back on such an argument.

Naturally I had other reasons. But I persisted in making *Seraphita* my advocate. Why? I tried to get to the bottom of it. Finally I grew ashamed of myself. Why did I have to justify myself? Why make excuses? The man was starving. He was ill. He was penniless. He was at the end of his rope. Weren't these reason enough? To be sure, he had been a pauper, a miserable pauper, all the years I had known him. The war hadn't changed anything; it had only rendered his situation more hopeless. But why quibble about his being an intimate friend or just a friend? Even if he had been a stranger, the fact that he was throwing himself on my mercy was enough. One doesn't let a drowning man sink.

"I've just got to do it!" I exclaimed. "I don't know how I'm going to do it, but I will. I'm writing him today." And then, to throw her a bone, I added: "Perhaps he won't like the idea."

"Don't worry," she said, "he'll grab at a straw."

So I wrote and explained the whole situation to him. I even drew a diagram of the place, giving the dimensions of his room, the fact that it was without heat, and adding that we were far from any city. "You may find it very dull here," I said, "with no one to talk to but us, no library to go to, no cafés, and the nearest cinema forty miles away. But at least you will not have to worry anymore about food and shelter." I concluded by saying that once here he would be his own master, could devote his time to whatever pleased him, in fact he could loaf the rest of his days away, if that was his wish.

He wrote back immediately, telling me that he was overjoyed, calling me a saint and a savior, et cetera, et cetera.

The next few months were consumed in raising the necessary funds. I borrowed whatever I could, diverted what few francs I had to his account, borrowed in advance on my royalties, and finally made definite arrangements for him to fly from Switzerland to England, there take the *Queen Mary* or *Elizabeth*, whichever it was, to New York, and fly from New York to San Francisco, where I would pick him up.

During these few months when we were borrowing and scraping I managed to maintain him in better style. He had to be fattened up or I would have an invalid on my hands. There was just one item I had failed to settle satisfactorily, that was to liquidate his back rent. The best I could do, under the circumstances, was to

23

send a letter which he was to show his landlady, a letter in which I promised to wipe out his debt just as soon as I possibly could. I gave her my word of honor.

Just before leaving he dispatched a last letter. It was to reassure me that, as regards the landlady, everything was jake. To allay her anxiety, he wrote, he had reluctantly given her a lay. Of course he couched it in more elegant terms. But he made it clear that, disgusting though it was, he had done his duty.

It was just a few days before Christmas when he landed at the airport in San Francisco. Since my car had broken down I asked my friend Lilik (Schatz) to meet him and put him up at his home in Berkeley until I could come and fetch him.

As soon as Moricand stepped off the plane he heard his name being called. "Monsieur Moricand! Monsieur Moricand! *Attention!*" He stopped dead and listened with open mouth. A beautiful contralto voice was speaking to him over the air in excellent French, telling him to step to the information desk, where someone was waiting for him.

He was dumbfounded. What a country! What service! For a moment he felt like a potentate.

It was Lilik who was waiting for him at the information desk. Lilik who had coached the girl. Lilik who whisked him away, fixed him a good meal, sat up with him until dawn and plied him with the best Scotch he could buy. And to top it off he had given him a picture of Big Sur which made it sound like the paradise which it is. He was a happy man, Conrad Moricand, when he finally hit the hay.

In a way, it worked out better than if I had gone to meet him myself.

When a few days passed and I found myself still unable to get to San Francisco, I telephoned Lilik and asked him to drive Moricand down.

They arrived the next day about nine in the evening.

I had gone through so many inner convulsions prior to his

24

arrival that when I opened the door and watched him descend the garden steps I was virtually numb. (Besides, the Capricorn seldom reveals his feelings all at once.)

As for Moricand, he was visibly moved. As we pulled away from an embrace I saw two big tears roll down his cheeks. He was "home" at last. Safe, sound, secure.

The little studio which I had turned over to him to sleep and work in was about half the size of his attic room in the Hotel Modial. It was just big enough to hold a cot, a writing table, a chiffonier. When the two oil lamps were lit it gave off a glow. A Van Gogh would have found it charming.

I could not help but notice how quickly he had arranged everything in his customary neat, orderly way. I had left him alone for a few minutes to unpack his bags and say an Ave Maria. When I returned to say goodnight I saw the writing table arranged as of yore—the large blotting pad resting slantwise on the triangular ruler, the block of paper resting slantwise on the triangular ruler, pen together with an assortment of pencils, all sharpened to a fine point. On the dresser, which had a mirror affixed to it, were laid out his comb and brush, his manicure scissors and nail file, a portable clock, his clothes brush and a pair of small framed photographs. He had already tacked up a few flags and pennants, just like a college boy. All that was missing to complete the picture was his birth chart.

I tried to explain how the Aladdin lamp worked, but it was too complicated for him to grasp all at once. He lit two candles instead. Then, apologizing for the close quarters he was to occupy, referring to it jokingly as a comfortable little tomb, I bade him goodnight. He followed me out to have a look at the stars and inhale a draught of clean, fragrant night air, assuring me that he would be perfectly comfortable in his cell.

When I went to call him the next morning I found him standing at the head of the stairs fully dressed. He was gazing out at the sea. The sun was low and bright in the sky, the atmosphere

25

extremely clear, the temperature that of a day in late spring. He seemed entranced by the vast expanse of the Pacific, by the far off horizon so sharp and clear, by the bright blue immensity of it all. A vulture hove into sight, made a low sweep in front of the house, then swooned away. He seemed stupefied by the sight. Then suddenly he realized how warm it was. "My God," he said, "and it is almost the first of January!"

"C'est un vrai paradis," he mumbled as he descended the steps.

Breakfast over, he showed me how to set and wind the clock which he had brought me as a gift. It was an heirloom, his last possession, he explained. It had been in the family for generations. Every quarter of an hour the chimes struck. Very softly, melodiously. He handled it with the utmost care while explaining at great length the complicated mechanism. He had even taken the precaution to look up a watch-maker in San Francisco, a reliable one, to whom I was to entrust the clock should anything go wrong with it.

I tried to express my appreciation of the marvelous gift he had made me, but somehow, deep inside, I was against the bloody clock. There was not a single possession of ours which was precious to me. Now I was saddled with an object which demanded care and attention. "A white elephant!" I said to myself. Aloud I suggested that he watch over it, regulate it, wind it, oil it, and so on. "You're used to it," I said. I wondered how long it would be before little Val—she was only a little over two—would begin tinkering with it in order to hear the music.

To my surprise, my wife did not find him too somber, too morbid, too aged, too decrepit. On the contrary, she remarked that he had a great deal of charm—and savoir-faire. She was rather impressed by his neatness and elegance. "Did you notice his hands? How beautiful! The hands of a musician." It was true, he had good strong hands with spatulate fingers and well-kept nails, which were always polished.

26

"Did you bring any old clothes?" I asked. He looked so citified in his dark business suit.

He had no old clothes, it turned out. Or rather he had the same good clothes which were neither new nor old. I noticed that he was eyeing me up and down with mild curiosity. I no longer owned a suit. I wore corduroy pants, a sweater with holes in it, somebody's hand-me-down jacket, and sneakers. My slouch hat—the last I was to own—had ventilators all around the sweat band. "One doesn't need clothes here," I remarked. "You can go naked, if you want."

"*Quelle vie!*" he exclaimed. "*C'est fantastique.*"

Later that morning, as he was shaving, he asked if I didn't have some talcum powder. "Of course," I said, and handed him the can I used. "Do you by chance have any Yardley?" he asked. "No," I said, "why?"

He gave me a strange, half-girlish, half-guilty smile. "I can't use anything but Yardley. Maybe when you go to town again you can get me some, yes?"

Suddenly it seemed as if the ground opened under my feet. Here he was, safe and secure, with a haven for the rest of his life in the midst of "*un vrai paradis,*" and he must have Yardley's talcum powder! Then and there I should have obeyed my instinct and said: "Beat it! Get back to your Purgatory!"

It was a trifling incident and, had it been any other man, I would have dismissed it immediately, put it down as a caprice, a foible, an idiosyncrasy, anything but an ominous presage. But of that instant I knew my wife was right, knew that I had made a grave mistake. In that moment I sensed the leech that Anaïs had tried to get rid of. I saw the spoiled child, the man who had never done an honest stroke of work in his life, the destitute individual who was too proud to beg openly but was not above milking a friend dry. I knew it all, felt it all, and already foresaw the end.

Each day I endeavored to reveal some new aspect of the region to him. There were the sulphur baths, which he found marvelous

27

—better than a European spa because natural, primitive, unspoiled. There was the "virgin forest" hard by, which he soon explored on his own, enchanted by the redwoods, the madrones, the wild flowers and the luxuriant ferns. Enchanted even more by what he called "neglect," for there are no forests in Europe which have the unkempt look of our American forests. He could not get over the fact that no one came to take the dead limbs and trunks which were piled crisscross above one another on either side of the trail. So much firewood going to waste! So much building material lying unused, unwanted, and the men and women of Europe crowded together in miserable little rooms without heat. "What a country!" he exclaimed. "Everywhere there is abundance. No wonder the Americans are so generous!"

My wife was not a bad cook. In fact, she was a rather good cook. There was always plenty to eat and sufficient wine to wash the food down. California wines, to be sure, but he thought them excellent, better in fact than the *vin rouge ordinaire* one gets in France. But there was one thing about the meals which he found difficult to adjust to—the absence of soup with each meal. He also missed the suite of courses which is customary in France. He found it hard to accommodate himself to a light lunch, which is the American custom. Midday was the time for the big meal. Our big meal was at dinner. Still, the cheeses weren't bad and the salads quite good, all things considered, though he would have preferred *l'huile d'arachide* (peanut oil) to the rather copious use of olive oil which we indulged in. He was glad we used garlic liberally. As for the *bifteks*, never had he eaten the like abroad. Now and then we dug up a little cognac for him, just to make him feel more at home.

But what bothered him most was our American tobacco. The cigarettes in particular were atrocious. Was it not possible to dig up some *gauloises bleues*, perhaps in San Francisco or New York? I opined that it was indeed but that they would be expensive. I suggested that he try Between the Acts. (Meanwhile, without telling him, I begged my friends in the big cities to rustle up some

28

French cigarettes.) He found the little cigars quite smokable. They reminded him of something even more to his liking—cheroots. I dug up some Italian stogies next time I went to town. Just ducky! Good! We're getting somewhere, thought I to myself.

One problem we hadn't yet solved was stationery. He had need, he maintained, for paper of a certain size. He showed me a sample which he had brought with him from Europe. I took it to town to see if it could be matched. Unfortunately it couldn't. It was an odd size, a size we had no demand for apparently. He found it impossible to believe that such could be the case. America made everything, and in abundance. Strange that one couldn't match an ordinary piece of paper. He grew quite incensed about it. Holding up the sample sheet, flicking it with his fingernail, he exclaimed: "Anywhere in Europe one can find this paper, exactly this size. And in America, which has everything, it can't be found. *C'est emmerdant!*"

To be frank, it was shitty to me too, the bloody subject. What could he be writing that demanded the use of paper precisely that size? I had got him his Yardley talc, his *gauloises bleues*, his eau de cologne, his powdered, slightly perfumed pumice stone (for a dentifrice), and now he was plaguing me about paper.

"Step outside a moment, won't you?" I begged. I spoke quietly, gently, soothingly. "Look out there . . look at that ocean! Look at the sky!" I pointed to the flowers which were in bloom. A hummingbird had just made as if to alight on the rose bush in front of us. All its motors were whirring. *"Regardez-moi ça!"* I exclaimed. I allowed a due pause. Then, in a very even tone of voice I said: "When a man has all this, can he not write just as well on toilet paper if he has to?"

It registered.

"Mon vieux," he began, "I hope you don't think I am exigent...."

"I do indeed," said I.

"You must forgive me. I'm sorry. Nobody could be more grateful than I for all you have done."

29

"My dear Moricand, I am not asking for gratitude. I'm asking for a little common sense." (I wanted to say "horse sense" but couldn't think of the equivalent in French immediately.) "Even if we had no paper at all I would expect you to be happy. You're a free man now, do you realize that? Why, god-damn it, you're better off than I am! Look, let's not spoil all this"—I gestured loosely toward the sky, the ocean, the birds of the air, the green hills—"let's not spoil all this with talk of paper, cigarettes, talcum powder and such nonsense. What we should be talking about is—*God*."

He was crestfallen. I felt like apologizing then and there, but I didn't. Instead I strode off in the direction of the forest. In the cool depths I sat down beside a pool and proceeded to give myself what the French call an *examen de conscience*. I tried to reverse the picture, put myself in his boots, look at myself through *his* eyes. I didn't get very far, I must confess. Somehow, I just could not put myself in his boots.

"Had my name been Moricand," said I softly to myself, "I would have killed myself long ago."

In one respect he was an ideal house guest—he kept to himself most of the day. Apart from meal times, he remained in his room almost the entire day, reading, writing, perhaps meditating too. I worked in the studio-garage just above him. At first the sound of my typewriter going full blast bothered him. It was like the rat-a-tat-tat of a machine gun in his ears. But gradually he got used to it, even found it stimulating, he said. At lunch and dinner he relaxed. Being so much on his own, he seized these occasions to engage us in conversation. He was the kind of talker it is diffi-cult to disengage once he has sunk his hooks into you. Lunch times I would often pull myself away abruptly, leaving him to work it out as best he could with my wife. Time is the one thing I regard as precious. If I had to waste time, I preferred to waste it in taking a nap rather than in listening to my friend Moricand. Dinner was another matter. It was hard to find an excuse for

30

terminating these sessions at my own time. It would have been a pleasure to glance at a book after dinner, since there was never any time for reading during the day, but I never got the chance. Once we were seated for the evening meal we were in for it till he had exhausted himself. Naturally, our conversations were all in French. Moricand had intended to learn a little English but after a few attempts gave it up. It was not a "sympathetic" language to him. It was even worse than German, he thought. Fortunately, my wife spoke some French and understood a lot more, but not enough to follow a man with Moricand's gift of speech. I couldn't always follow him myself. Every now and then I would have to halt the flow, ask him to repeat what he had just said in simpler language, then translate it for my wife. Now and then I would forget myself and give him a spate of English, soon arrested of course by his blank look. To translate these bursts was like sweating out a cold. If, as frequently happened, I had to explain something to my wife in English, he would pretend that he understood. She would do the same when he conveyed something confidential to me in French. Thus it happened that often the three of us were talking three different subjects, nodding, agreeing with one another, saying Yes when we meant No, and so on, until the confusion became so great that we all threw up our hands simultaneously. Then we would begin all over, sentence by sentence, thought by thought, as if struggling to cement a piece of string.

Nevertheless, and despite all frustration, we managed to understand one another exceedingly well. Usually it was only in the long, overembroidered monologue that we lost him. Even then, astray in the complicated web of a long-drawn-out story or a windy explanation of some hermeneutic point, it was a pleasure to listen to him. Sometimes I would deliberately let go my attention, facilitate the process of getting lost, in order to better enjoy the music of his words. At his best he was a one man orchestra.

It made no difference, when he was in the groove, what he chose to talk about—food, costume, ritual, pyramids, Trismegistus or

Eleusinian mysteries. Any theme served as a means to exploit his virtuosity. In love with all that is subtle and intricate, he was always lucid and convincing. He had a feminine flair for preciosities, could always produce the exact timbre, shade, nuance, odor, taste. He had the suavity, velleity and mellifluousness of an enchanter. And he could put into his voice a resonance comparable in effect to the sound of a gong reverberating in the deathlike silence of a vast desert. If he spoke of Odilon Redon, for example, his language reeked of fragrant colors, of exquisite and mysterious harmonies, of alchemical vapors and imaginings, of pensive broodings and spiritual distillations too impalpable to be fixed in words but which words could evoke or suggest when marshaled in sensorial patterns. There was something of the harmonium in the use he made of his voice. It was suggestive of some intermediate region, the confluence, say, of divine and mundane streams where form and spirit interpenetrated, and which could only be conveyed musically. The gestures accompanying this music were limited and stereotyped, mostly facial movements—sinister, vulgarly accurate, diabolical when restricted to the mouth and lips, poignant, pathetic, harrowing, when concentrated in the eyes. Shudderingly effective when he moved his whole scalp. The rest of him, his body, one might say, was usually immobile, except for a slight tapping or drumming with the fingers now and then. Even his intelligence seemed to be centered in the sound box, the harmonium which was situated neither in the larynx nor in the chest but in a middle region which corresponded to the locus empyrean whence he drew his imagery.

Staring at him abstractly in one of those fugitive moments when I caught myself wandering among the reeds and bulrushes of my own vagaries, I would find myself studying him as if through a reflector, his image changing, shifting like swift-moving cloud formations: now the sorrowful sage, now the sybil, now the grand cosmocrator, now the alchemist, now the stargazer, now the mage. Sometimes he looked Egyptian, sometimes Mongolian,

32

sometimes Iroquois or Mohican, sometimes Chaldean, sometimes Etruscan. Often very definite figures out of the past leaped to mind, figures he either seemed to incarnate momentarily or figures he had affinities with. To wit: Montezuma, Herod, Nebuchadnez-zar, Ptolemy, Balthasar, Justinian, Solon. Revelatory names, in a way. However conglomerate, in essence they served to coalesce certain elements of his nature which ordinarily defied association. He was an alloy, and a very strange one at that. Not bronze, not brass, not electrum. Rather some nameless colloidal sort of alloy such as we associate with the body when it becomes a prey to some rare disease.

There was one image he bore deep within him, one he had created in youth and which he was never to shake off: "Gloomy Gus." The day he showed me a photograph of himself at the age of fifteen or sixteen I was profoundly disturbed. It was almost an exact replica of my boyhood friend, Gus Schmelzer, whom I used to tease and plague beyond endurance because of his somber, morose, eternally somber and morose mien. Even at that age—perhaps earlier, who knows?—there were engraved in Moricand's psyche all the modalities which such terms as lunar, saturnian and sepulchral evoke. One could already sense the mummy which the flesh would become. One could see the bird of ill omen perched on his left shoulder. One could feel the moonlight altering his blood, sensitizing his retina, dyeing his skin with the pallor of the prisoner, the drug addict, the dweller on forbidden planets. Know-ing him, one might even visualize those delicate antennae of which he was altogether too proud and on which he placed a reliance which overtaxed his intuitive muscles, so to speak. I might go further—why not?—and say that, looking deep into his sorrow-ful eyes, somber, simian eyes, I could see skull within skull, an endless, cavernous Golgotha illumined by the dry, cold, murderous light of a universe beyond the imaginative bounds of even the hardiest scientific dreamer.

In the art of resuscitation he was a master. Touching anything that smacked of death, he came alive. Everything filtered through to him from the tomb in which it was buried. He had only to wave his wand to create the semblance of life. But, as with all sorcery, even the most poetic, the end was always dust and ashes. For Moricand the past was rarely a living past; it was a morgue which at best could be made to resemble a museum. Even his description of the living was but a cataloguing of museum pieces. There was no distinction in his enthusiasms between that which is and that which was. Time was his medium. A deathless medium which had no relation to life.

It is said that Capricorns get on well together, presumably because they have so much in common. It is my own belief that there are more divergences among these earth-bound creatures, that they have more difficulty understanding one another, than is the case with other types. Mutual understanding between Capricorns is more a surface agreement, a truce, so to speak, than anything else. At home in the depths or on the heights, seldom inhabiting any region for long, they have more kinship with the roc and the leviathan than with one another. What they do understand, perhaps, is that their differences are altitudinal, due primarily to shifts of position. Capable of running the whole gamut, it is easy for them to identify as you or me. This is their bond and explains their ability to forgive but never to forget. They forget nothing, ever. Their memory is phantasmagorical. They remember not only their personal, human tribulations, but their prehuman and subhuman ones as well. They can slither back into the protoplasmic slime with the ease of eels slipping through mud. They also carry remembrances of higher spheres, of seraphic states, as if they had known long periods of liberation from earthly thralls, as if the very language of the seraphim were familiar to them. Indeed, one might almost say of them that it is earthly existence to which they, the earth-bound, are of all types least suited. To them the earth is not only a prison, a purgatory, a place of expiation but it is also a cocoon from which they will eventually escape

34

equipped with indestructible wings. Hence their mediumship, their ability and desire to practice acceptance, their extraordinary readiness for conversion. They enter the world like visitors destined for another planet, another sphere. Their attitude is one of having a last look around, of perpetually bidding good-bye to all that is terrestrial. They imbibe the very essence of the earth, and in doing so prepare the new body, the new form, in which they will take leave of earth forever. They die innumerable deaths whereas others die but once. Hence their immunity to life *or* death. Their true locus is the heart of mystery. There all is clear to them. There they live apart, spin their dreams, and are "at home."

He was hardly with us more than a week when he called me to his cell one day for a "consultation." It was about the uses of codeine. Beginning with a long preamble about his sufferings and privations since the year one, he ended with a brief account of the nightmare he had lived through during his recent sojourn in Switzerland. Though he was a Swiss citizen, Switzerland was not his country, not his climate, not his bowl of soup. After all the humiliations he had suffered during the war (the second one) came even worse ones which the unfeeling Swiss had imposed. All this by way of leading up to the seven-year itch. He paused to roll up his trousers. I was horrified. His legs were nothing but a mass of sores. There was no need to dwell further on the subject.

Now if he could only get a little codeine, he explained, it would help to calm his nerves, allow him to get some sleep at least, even though it could not cure the itch. Wouldn't I try to get some for him, perhaps tomorrow when I went to town? I said I would.

I had never used codeine or any drug that puts one to sleep or wakes one up. I had no idea that codeine could only be had by doctor's prescription. It was the druggist who informed me of this. Not wishing to disappoint Moricand, I called on two doctors I knew to ask if they would furnish me with the necessary prescription. They refused.

35

When I informed Moricand of the situation he was almost beside himself. He acted as if there were a conspiracy on the part of American physicians to keep him in misery. "How absurd!" he cried. "Even in Switzerland it's sold openly. I would have more chance, I suppose, if I asked for cocaine or opium."

Another day or two passed, during which time he got no sleep at all. Then another consultation. This time to inform me that he had thought of a way out. Very simple, too. He would write to his druggist in Switzerland and ask him to mail him the codeine in very small particles. I explained to him that such importation would be illegal, no matter how small the quantity. I explained further that he would be incriminating me too should he do such a thing.

"What a country! What a country!" he exclaimed, raising his hands heavenward.

"Why don't you try the baths again?" I suggested. He promised he would. He said it as if I had requested him to swallow a dose of castor oil.

As I was about to leave he showed me a letter which he had just received from his landlady. It was about the bill he owed and my failure to keep my promise. I had completely forgotten about her and her bloody bill.

We never had any money in the bank, but I did have a few bills in my pocket. I fished them out. "Maybe this will quiet her for a while," I said, laying them on his table.

About a week later he called me to his room again. He was holding an envelope in his hand which he had just opened. He wanted me to look at the contents. It was a letter from his Swiss druggist say that he was happy to be of service. I looked up and saw the tiny pellets which he was holding in the palm of his hand.

"You see," he said, "there is always a way."

I was furious but tongue-tied. I could not deny that, were the situation reversed, I would probably have done the same. He was desperate, that was obvious. Besides, the baths had been no help. He was

They had aggravated his condition, if I was to believe him. At any rate, he was through with the baths: they were poison to his system.

Now that he had what he needed he took to roaming the forest regularly. Good, thought I, he needs the exercise. But he overdid it; the excessive walking made his blood boil. From another standpoint these excursions did him good. The forest bequeathed something which his Swiss spirit demanded. He always returned from his walks elated and physically exhausted. "Tonight," he would say, "I should be able to sleep without taking any pills."

He deceived himself. The itching grew worse. He continued to scratch himself furiously, even in deep slumber. The itch had traveled too. Now it had attacked his arms. Soon it would devastate his whole body, all but his genitals.

There were remissions, of course. If guests arrived, particularly French-speaking guests, his morale improved overnight. Or if he received a letter from a dear friend who was still doing a stretch in prison because of his activities during the Occupation. Sometimes an exceptionally good dinner was sufficient to change his mood for a day or two. The itching never ceased, apparently, but the scratching might be halted for a while.

As the days passed, he became more and more aware that I was a person upon whom it gave people pleasure to shower gifts. With the mail there came packages containing all manner of things. What astounded Moricand was that they were usually the very things we were in need of. If we ran out of wine a friend was sure to turn up with an armful of excellent bottles; if I needed wood, a neighbor would appear with the gift of a load of wood, enough to last several months. Books and magazines, of course, poured in steadily. Now and then I would receive postage stamps, whole sheets of them. Only money failed to pour in. That always came in a trickle, a trickle which often dried up altogether.

It was with a falcon's eye that Moricand eyed this steady influx of gifts. As for the steady flow of visitors, even the bores, the time

37

wasters, he observed, were instrumental in lightening our burdens. "It's altogether natural," he would say. "It's there in your horoscope. Even when Jupiter deserts you at times you are never left unprotected. Besides, with *you* misfortune only works to your ultimate advantage. You can't possibly lose!"

I never dreamed of responding to such remarks by pointing out the struggles and the sacrifices I had made throughout my life. But to myself I would say: "It's one thing for 'it' to be in your horoscope; it's another to make it manifest."

One thing seemed to escape his notice entirely—the favors, the services which my friends were constantly rendering him. He had not the slightest notion how much everyone was concerned for his welfare. He behaved as if it were all a matter of course, now that he was in the land of plenty. Americans were like that, naturally kind and generous, don't you know. They were born lucky, the gods looked after them. A shade of contempt always crept into his voice when he referred to the benevolence of the American. He lumped us with the huge cauliflowers, carrots, squash and other monstrous-looking vegetables and fruits we produce in inexhaustible quantity.

I had asked only one little favor of Moricand when I invited him to stay with us for the rest of his days. That was to teach my daughter French, if possible. I had asked it more to relieve him of an undue sense of gratitude than for any deep concern about the child's acquisition of French. All she ever learned during his stay with us was *Oui* and *Non*, and *Bon jour, Monsieur Moricand!* He seemed to have no use for children; they annoyed him, unless they were extremely well behaved. As with most people who stress behavior, being well behaved meant keeping out of sight and reach. He was utterly at a loss to understand my preoccupation with the child, the daily walks we took, the efforts I made to amuse, entertain and instruct her, the patience with which I listened to her idiotic questions, her excessive demands. He had no idea, naturally, of the joy she gave me. It was obvious, but perhaps he did not wish to recognize it, that she was my only joy. Val always came first. It irritated everyone, not only Moricand. And particularly my wife. The opinion roundabout was that I was an aging dolt who was spoiling his only child. Outwardly it did indeed seem so. The reality which underlay the situation, or the relationship, I hesitated to reveal even to my intimate friends. It was ironic, to be sure, that the very ones who levelled these reproaches were guilty of doing the same silly things, of showing the same exaggerated affection, for their pets. As for Val, she was my own flesh and blood, the apple of my eye; my only regret was that I could not give her more time and attention.

It was about this time that the little mothers all became interested in the dance. Some went in for singing too. Very fine. Commendable, as we say. But what about the children? Were they also taught to sing and dance? Not a bit. That would come later, when they were old enough to be sent to the ballet class or whatever the fad might be which the little mothers deemed indispensable in the cultural advancement of their progeny. The mothers were too busy at the moment cultivating their own latent talents.

There came a day when I taught Val her first song. We were marching home through the woods; I had hoisted her on my shoulders to save her weary little legs. Suddenly she asked me to sing. "What would you like?" I said, and then I gave her that feeble joke of Abraham Lincoln about knowing only two songs: one was "Yankee Doodle," the other wasn't.

"Sing it!" she begged.

I did, and with a vengeance. She joined in. By the time we arrived home she knew the verse by heart. I was supremely delighted. We had to sing it over and over, naturally. It was Yankee Doodle this and Yankee Doodle that. Yankee Doodle dandy and the Devil take the hindmost!

Moricand took not the slightest interest in such diversions. "Poor Miller!" he probably said to himself, meaning what a ridiculous figure I could cut.

39

Poor Val! How it cut me when, endeavoring to have a few words with him, she would get for rebuff: "I speak no English." At table she annoyed him incessantly with her silly chatter, which I found delicious, and her poor table manners.

"She ought to be disciplined," he would say. "It's not good for a child to receive so much attention."

My wife, being of the same mind, would chime in like a clock. She would bemoan the fact that I frustrated all her efforts in this direction, would make it appear that I took a diabolical pleasure in seeing the child misbehave. She could not admit, naturally, that her own spirit was of cast iron, that discipline was her only recourse.

"He believes in *freedom*," she would say, making the idea of freedom sound like utter rubbish.

To which Moricand would rejoin: "Yes, the American child is a little barbarian. In Europe the child knows its place. **Here the child rules.**"

All too true, alas! And yet. . . . What he forgot to add is what every intelligent European knows, what he himself knew only too well and had admitted many times, namely, that in Europe, especially *his* Europe, the child becomes an adult long before his time, that he is disciplined to death, that he is given an education which is not only "barbarous" but cruel, crazy, stultifying, that stern, disciplinary measures *may* make well-behaved children but seldom emancipated adults. **He** forgot, moreover, to say what his own childhood had been like, to explain what discipline, good manners, refinement, education had done for him.

To exculpate himself in *my* eyes he would wind up by explaining to my wife that I was a born anarchist, that my sense of freedom was a peculiarly personal one, that the very idea of discipline was abhorrent to my nature. I was a rebel and an outlaw, a spiritual freak, so to say. My function in life was to create disturbance. Adding very soberly that there was need for such as me. Then, as if carried away, he would proceed to rectify the picture. It **was** also a fact, he had to admit, that I was too good, too kind, too

40

gentle, too patient, too indulgent, too forbearing, too forgiving. As if this balanced the violence, the ruthlessness, the recklessness, the treachery of my essential being. At this point he might even say that I *was* capable of understanding discipline, since, as he put it, my ability to write was based on the strictest kind of self-discipline.

"C'est un être bien compliqué," he would conclude. "Fortunately, I understand him. I know him inside out." With this he would press his thumb against the table top, as if squashing a louse. That was *me* under his thumb, the anomaly which he had studied, analyzed, dissected, and could interpret when occasion demanded.

Often an evening that began auspiciously would end in an involved discussion of our domestic problems, something which I abhorred but which wives seem to enjoy, particularly when they have a sympathetic listener. Since I had long resigned myself to the futility of arriving at any understanding with my wife through discussion—I might as well have talked to a stone wall—I limited my participation to rectifying falsehoods and distortions of fact. For the most part I presented an adamant silence. Quite aware that there are always two sides to the picture, poor Moricand would struggle to shift the discussion to more fundamental grounds.

"One gets nowhere with a type like Miller," he would say to my wife. "He does not think in the way you and I do. He thinks in circular fashion. He has no logic, no sense of measure, he is contemptuous of reason and common sense."

He would then proceed to describe to her *her* virtues and defects, in order to demonstrate why we could never see eye to eye, she and I. "But I understand you both. I can act as arbiter. I know how to put the puzzle together."

As a matter of fact, he was quite correct in this. He proved to be a most excellent referee. In his presence, what might have ended in explosions ended only in tears or mute perplexity. Often, when I prayed that he would grow weary and take leave of us for the night, I could sense my wife doing the very opposite. Her only

41

chance of talking with me, or at me, was in his presence. Alone we were either at one another's throats or giving each other the silence. Moricand often succeeded in lifting these furious and prolonged arguments, which had become routine, to another level; he helped us, momentarily at least, to isolate our thoughts, survey them dispassionately, examine them from other angles, free them of their obsessive nature. It was on such occasions that he made good use of his astrological wisdom, for nothing can be more cool and objective, more soothing and staying to the victim of emotion, than the astrological picture of his plight.

Not every evening was spent in argument and discussion, to be sure. The best evenings were those in which we gave him free rein. After all, the monologue was his forte. If by chance we touched on the subject of painting—he had begun life as a painter —we were sure to be richly rewarded for hearing him out. Many of the now celebrated figures in French art he had known intimately. Some he had befriended in his days of opulence. His anecdotes concerning what I choose to call the golden period—the two or three decades leading up to the appearance of *les Fauves*— were delicious in the sense that a rich meal is delicious. They were always spiced with uncanny observations that did not lack a certain diabolical charm. For me this period was fraught with vital interest. I had always felt that I was born twenty or thirty years too late, always regretted that I had not first visited Europe (and remained there) as a young man. Seen it *before* the First World War, I mean. What would I not give to have been the comrade or bosom friend of such figures as Apollinaire, Douanier Rousseau, George Moore, Max Jacob, Vlaminck, Utrillo, Derain, Cendrars, Gauguin, Modigliani, Cingria, Picabia, Maurice Magre, Léon Daudet, and such like. How much greater would have been the thrill to cycle along the Seine, cross and recross her bridges, race through towns like Bougival, Châtou, Argenteuil, Marly-le-roi, Puteaux, Rambouillet, Issy-les-Moulineaux and similar environs circa 1910 rather than the year 1932 or 1933! What a difference it

42

would have made to see Paris from the top of a horse-drawn omnibus at the age of twenty-one! Or to view the *grands boulevards* as a *flâneur* in the period made famous by the Impressionists!

Moricand could summon all the splendor and misery of this epoch at will. He could induce that *"nostalgie de Paris"* which Carco is so adept at, which Aragon, Léon-Paul Fargue, Daudet, Duhamel and so many French writers have given us time and again. It needed only the mention of a street name, a crazy monument, a restaurant or cabaret which exists no more, to start the wheels turning. His evocations were even more piquant to me because he had seen it all through the eyes of a snob. However much he had participated, he had never suffered as did the men he spoke of. His sufferings were to come only when those who had not been killed in the war or committed suicide or gone insane had become famous. Did he ever imagine in his days of opulence, I wonder, that the time would come when he would be obliged to beg his poor friend Max Jacob for a few sous—Max who had renounced the world and was living like an ascetic? A terrible thing to come down in the world when your old friends are rising on the horizon like stars, when the world itself, once a playground, has become a shabby carnival, a cemetery of dreams and illusions.

How he loathed the Republic and all it represented! Whenever he made mention of the French Revolution it was as if he were face to face with evil itself. Like Nostradamus, he dated the deterioration, the blight, the downfall from the day *le peuple—la canaille,* in other words—took over. It is strange, now that I come to think of it, that he never once spoke of Gilles de Rais. Any more than he ever spoke of Ramakrishna, Milarepa, or St. Francis. Napoleon, yes. Bismarck, yes. Voltaire, yes. Villon, yes. And Pythagoras, of course. The whole Alexandrian world was as familiar and vivid to him as if he had known it in a previous incarnation. The Manichean world of thought was also a reality to him. Of Zoroastrian teachings he dwelt by predilection on that aspect which proclaims "the reality of evil." Possibly he also believed

43

that Ormuzd would eventually prevail over Ahriman, but if so it was an eventuality only realizable in a distant future, a future so distant as to render all speculation about it, or even hope in it, futile. No, the reality of evil was undoubtedly the strongest conviction he held. He was so aware of it, indeed, that he could enjoy nothing to the full; actively or passively he was always exorcising the evil spirits which pervade every phase, rung and sphere of life.

One evening, when we had touched on things close to his heart, he asked me suddenly if I had lost all interest in astrology. "You never mention it any more," he said.

"True," I replied. "I don't see what it would serve me to pursue it further. I was never interested in it the way you are. For me it was just another language to learn, another keyboard to manipulate. It's only the poetic aspect of anything which really interests me. In the ultimate there is only one language—the language of truth. It matters little how we arrive at it."

I forget what his reply to this was precisely, only that it conveyed a veiled reproach for my continued interest in Oriental thought. I was too absorbed in abstract speculations, he hinted. Too Germanic, possibly. The astrologic approach was a corrective I stood in need of. It would help to integrate, orient, and organize much in me that was *flou* and chaotic. There was always a danger, with a type like me, of becoming either a saint or a fanatic.

"Not a lunatic, eh?"

"Jamais!"

"But something of a fool! Is that it?"

His answer was—Yes and No. I had a strong religious strain, a metaphysical bent. There was more than a touch of the Crusader in me. I was both humble and arrogant, a penitent and an Inquisitioner. And so on.

"And you think a deeper knowledge of astrology would help overcome these tendencies?"

"I would not put it exactly like that," he said. "I would say simply that it would help you to see more clearly . . . see into the nature of your problems."

44

"But I have no problems," I replied. "Unless they are cosmological ones. I am at peace with myself—and with the world. It's true, I don't get along with my wife. But neither did Socrates, for that matter. Or . . ."

He stopped me.

"All right," I said, "tell me this—what has astrology done for *you?* Has it enabled you to correct your defects? Has it helped you to adjust to the world? Has it given you peace and joy? Why do you scratch yourself like a madman?"

The look he gave me was enough to tell me that I had hit below the belt.

"I'm sorry," I said, "but you know that I'm often rude and direct for a good reason. I don't mean to belittle you or make fun of you. But here's what I would like to know. Answer me straight! What is the most important—peace and joy or wisdom? If to know less would make you a happier man, which would you choose?"

I might have known his answer. It was that we have no choice in such matters.

I violently disagreed. "Perhaps," said I, "I am still very much of an American. That is to say, naive, optimistic, gullible. Perhaps all I gained from the fruitful years I spent in France was a strengthening and deepening of my own inner spirit. In the eyes of a European, what am I but an American to the core, an American who exposes his Americanism like a sore. Like it or not, I am a product of this land of plenty, a believer in superabundance, a believer in miracles. Any deprivation I suffered was my own doing. I blame nobody but myself for my woes and afflictions, for my shortcomings, for my transgressions. What you believe I might have learned through a deeper knowledge of astrology I learned through experience of life. I made all the mistakes that it is possible for a man to make—and I paid the penalty. I am that much richer, that much wiser, that much happier, if I may say so, than if I had found through study or through discipline how to avoid the snares and pitfalls in my path. . . . Astrology deals in potentialities, does it not? I am not interested in the potential man. I

45

am interested in what a man actualizes—or realizes—of his potential being. And what is the potential man, after all? Is he not the sum of all that is human? *Divine*, in other words? You think I am searching for God. I am not. God is. The world is. Man is. We are. The full reality, that's God—and man, and the world, and all that is, including the unnameable. I'm for reality. More and more reality. I'm a fanatic about it, if you like. And what is astrology? What has it to do with reality? Something, to be sure. So has astronomy, so has biology, so has mathematics, so has music, so has literature; and so have the cows in the field and the flowers and the weeds, and the manure that brings them back to life. In some moods some things seem more important than others. Some things have value, others don't, we say. *Everything* is important and of value. Look at it that way and I'll accept your astrology...."

"You're in one of your moods again," he said, shrugging his shoulders.

"I know it," I replied. "Just be patient with me. You'll have your turn. . . . Every so often I revolt, even against what I believe in with all my heart. I have to attack everything, myself included. Why? To simplify things. We know too much—and too little. It's the intellect which gets us into trouble. Not our intelligence. *That* we can never have enough of. But I get weary of listening to specialists, weary of listening to the man with one string to his fiddle. I don't deny the validity of astrology. What I object to is becoming enslaved to any one point of view. Of course there are affinities, analogies, correspondences, a heavenly rhythm and an earthly rhythm . . . *as above, so below*. It would all be crazy if it weren't so. But knowing it, accepting it, why not forget it? I mean, make it a living part of one's life, something absorbed, assimilated and distributed through every pore of one's being, and thus forgotten, altered, utilized in the spirit and the service of life. I abhor people who have to filter everything through the one language they know, whether it be astrology, religion, yoga, politics, economics or what. The one thing about this uni-

46

verse of ours which intrigues me, which makes me realize that it *is* divine and beyond all knowing, is that it lends itself so easily to any and all interpretations. Everything we formulate about it is correct and incorrect at the same time. It includes our truths and our errors. And, whatever we think about the universe in no way alters it. . . .

"Let me get back to where I started. We all have different lives to lead. We all want to make conditions as smooth and harmonious for ourselves as possible. We all want to extract the full measure of life. Must we go to books and teachers, to science, religion, philosophy, must we know so much—and so little!—to take the path? Can we not become fully awake and aware without the torture we put ourselves through?"

"Life is nothing but a Calvary," he said. "Not even a knowledge of astrology can alter that stern fact."

"What about the exceptions? Surely. . . ."

"There are no exceptions," he replied. "Everyone, even the most enlightened, has his private griefs and torments. Life is perpetual struggle, and struggle entails sorrow and suffering. And suffering gives us strength and character."

"For what? To what end?"

"The better to endure life's burdens."

"What a woeful picture! It's like training for a contest in which one knows in advance he will be defeated."

"There is such a thing as renunciation," he said.

"But is it a solution?"

"For some Yes, for others No. Sometimes one has no choice."

"In your honest opinion, do we ever really have what is called choice?"

He thought a moment before answering.

"Yes, I believe we do have a measure of choice, but much less than people think. Within the limits of our destiny we are free to choose. It is here precisely that astrology is of great importance: when you realize the conditions under which you have come into

47

the world, which astrology makes clear, you do not choose the unchooseable."

"The lives of great men," said I, "would seem to tell us the opposite."

"As you say, *so it would seem*. But if one examines their horoscopes one is impressed by the fact that they could scarcely have chosen other than they did. What one chooses or wills is always in accordance with one's character. Faced with the same dilemma, a Napoleon would act one way, and a St. Paul another."

"Yes, yes, I know all that," I interrupted. "And I also know, or believe, that St. Francis would have been St. Francis, St. Paul St. Paul, and Napoleon Napoleon, even if they had had a profound knowledge of astrology. To understand one's problems, to be able to look into them more deeply, to eliminate the unnecessary ones, none of that really interests me any longer. Life as a burden, life as a battleground, life as a problem—these are all partial ways of looking at life. Two lines of poetry often tell us more, give us more, than the weightiest tome by an erudite. To make anything truly significant one has to poetize it. The only way I get astrology, or anything else, for that matter, is as poetry, as music. If the astrological view brings out new notes, new harmonies, new vibrations, it has served its purpose—for me. Knowledge weighs one down; wisdom saddens one. The love of truth has nothing to do with knowledge or wisdom: it's beyond their domains. Whatever certitude one possesses is beyond the realm of proof.

"The saying goes, 'It takes all kinds to make a world.' Precisely. The same does not hold for views or opinions. Put all the pictures together, all the views, all the philosophies, and you do not get a totality. The sum of all these angles of visions do not and never will make truth. The sum of all knowledge is greater confusion. The intellect runs away with itself. Mind is not intellect. The intellect is a product of the ego, and the ego can never be stilled, never be satisfied. When do we begin to know that we know?"

When we have ceased to believe that we can ever know. Truth comes with surrender. And it's wordless. The brain is not the mind; it is a tyrant which seeks to dominate the mind.

"What has all this to do with astrology? Nothing perhaps, and yet everything. To you I am an illustration of a certain kind of Capricorn; to an analyst I'm something else; to a Marxist another kind of specimen, and so on. What's all that to *me?* What does it concern me how your photographic apparatus registers? To see a person whole and for what he is one has to use another kind of camera; one has to have an eye that is even more objective than the camera's lens. One has to see through the various facets whose brilliant reflections blind us to the real nature of an individual. The more we learn the less we know; the more equipment we have the less we are able to see. It's only when we stop trying to see, stop trying to know, that we really see and know. What sees and knows has no need of spectacles and theories. All our striving and struggling is in the nature of confession. It is a way of reminding ourselves that we are weak, ignorant, blind, helpless. Whereas we are *not.* We are as little or as much as we permit ourselves to think we are.

"Sometimes I think that astrology must have had its inception at a moment in man's evolution when he lost faith in himself. Or, to put it another way, when he lost his wholeness. When he wanted to know instead of to be. Schizophrenia began far back, not yesterday or the day before. And when man split he split into myriad fragments. But even today, as fragmented as he is, he can be made whole again. The only difference between the Adamic man and the man of today is that the one was born to Paradise and the other has to create it. And that brings me back to the question of choice. A man can only prove that he is free by electing to be so. And he can only do so when he realizes that he himself made himself unfree. And that to me means that he must wrest from God the powers he has given God. The more of God he recognizes in himself the freer he becomes. And the

49

freer he becomes the fewer decisions he has to make, the less choice is presented to him. Freedom is a misnomer. Certitude is more like it. Unerringness. Because truthfully there is always only one way to act in any situation, not two, nor three. Freedom implies choice and choice exists only to the extent that we are aware of our ineptitude. The adept takes no thought, one might say. He is one with though, one with the path.

"It seems as if I were straying far afield. I'm not, really. I'm merely talking another language. I'm saying that peace and joy is within everyone's province. I'm saying that our essential being is godlike. I'm saying. I'm saying that there are no limitations, either to thought or action. I'm saying that we're one, not many. I'm saying that we are there, that we never could be anywhere else except through negation. I'm saying that to see differences is to make differences. A Capricorn is a Capricorn only to another astrologer. Astrology makes use of a few planets, of the sun and the moon, but what of the millions of other planets, other universes, all the stars, the comets, the meteors, the asteroids? Does distance count, or size, or radiance? Is not all one, interactive, interpenetrating? Who dares to say where influences begin and leave off? Who dares to say what is important and what is not? Who owns this universe? Who regulates it? Whose spirit informs it? If we need help, guidance, directions, why not go straight to the source? And what do we want help, guidance and direction for? To make things more comfortable for ourselves, to be more efficient, to better achieve our ends? Why is everything so complicated, so difficult, so obscure, so unsatisfactory? Because we have made ourselves the center of the universe, because we want everything to work out as we wish it. What we need to discover is what *it* wishes, call *it* life, mind, God, whatever you please. If that is the purpose of astrology, I am all for it.

"There's something else I would like to say, to finish with the subject once and for all. It's about our everyday problems, principally the problem of getting along with one another, which

50

seems to be the main problem. What I say is, if we are going to meet one another with a view or an awareness of our diversity and divergences we will never acquire enough knowledge to deal with one another smoothly and effectively. To get anywhere with another individual one has to cut through to the rock-bottom man, to that common human substratum which exists in all of us. This is not a difficult procedure and certainly doesn't demand of one that he be a psychologist or a mind reader. One doesn't have to know a thing about astrological types, the complexity of their reactions to this or that. There is one simple, direct way to deal with all types, and that is truthfully and honestly. We spend our lives trying to avoid the injuries and humiliations which our neighbors may inflict upon us. A waste of time. If we abandoned fear and prejudice, we could meet the murderer as easily as the saint. I get fed up with astrological parlance when I observe people studying their charts to find a way out of illness, poverty, vice, or whatever it may be. To me it seems like a sorry attempt to exploit the stars. We talk about fate as if it were something visited upon us; we forget that we create our fate every day we live. And by fate I mean the woes that beset us, which are merely the effects of causes which are not nearly as mysterious as we pretend. Most of the ills we suffer from are directly traceable to our own behavior. Man is not suffering from the ravages wrought by earthquakes and volcanoes, by tornadoes and tidal waves; he is suffering from his own misdeeds, his own foolishness, his own ignorance and disregard of natural laws. Man can eliminate war, can eliminate disease, can eliminate old age and probably death too. He need not live in poverty, vice, ignorance, in rivalry and competition. All these conditions are within his province, within his power, to alter. But he can never alter them as long as he is concerned solely with his own individual fate. Imagine a physician refusing his services because of danger of infection or contamination! We are all members of the one body, as the Bible says. And we are all at war with one another. Our own physical body possesses a wisdom which we who inhabit the body lack. We give it orders which make no sense. There is no mystery about disease, nor crime, nor war, nor the thousand and one things which plague us. Live simply and wisely. Forget, forgive, renounce, abdicate. Do I need to study my horoscope to understand the wisdom of such simple behavior? Do I have to live with yesterday in order to enjoy tomorrow? Can I not scrap the past instantly, begin at once to live the good life—if I really mean to? *Peace and joy. . . .* I say it's ours for the asking. Day by day, that's good enough for me. Not even that, in fact. Just today! *Le bel aujourd'hui!* Wasn't that the title of one of Cendrars' books? Give me a better one, if you can. . . ."

Naturally, I did not deliver this harangue all in one breath, nor exactly in these words. Perhaps much of it I merely imagine that I said. No matter. I say it now as of then. It was all there in my mind, not once, but repeatedly. Take it for what it's worth.

With the coming of the first good rain he began to grow despondent. It's true that his cell was tiny, that water leaked through the roof and the windows, that the sow bugs and other bugs took over, that they often dropped on his bed when he was asleep, that to keep warm he had to use an ill-smelling oil stove which consumed what little oxygen remained after he had sealed up all the cracks and crevices, stuffed the space beneath the door with sacking, shut all the windows tight, and so on. It's true that it was a winter in which we got more than our usual share of rain, a winter in which the storms broke with fury and lasted for days on end. And he, poor devil, was cooped up all day, restless, ill at ease, either too hot or too cold, scratching, scratching, and utterly incapable of warding off the hundred and one abominations which materialized out of the ether, for how else explain the presence of all these creeping, crawling, ugly things when all had been shut tight, sealed and fumigated?

I shall never forget his look of utter bewilderment and distress when he called me to his room one late afternoon to inspect the lamps, "Look," he said, striking a match and applying the flame to the wick. "Look, it goes out every time."

Now Aladdin lamps are quixotic and temperamental, as country people know. They have to be kept in perfect condition to function properly. Just to trim the wick neatly is in itself a delicate operation. Of course I had explained things to him a number of times, but every time I visited him I noticed that the lamps were dim or smoking. I knew too that he was too annoyed with them to bother keeping them in condition.

Striking a match and holding it against the wick, I was just about to say, "You see, it's simple . . . nothing to it"—when, to my surprise, the wick refused to ignite. I lit another and another, and still the wick refused to take fire. It was only when I reached for a candle and saw how it spluttered that I realized what was wrong.

I opened the door to let in some air and then tried the lamp again. It worked. "Air, my friend. You need air!" He looked at me in amazement. To get air he would have to keep a window open. And that would let the wind and rain in. "*Cest emmerdant!*" he exclaimed. It was indeed. It was worse than that. I had visions of finding him in bed one fine morning—suffocated.

Eventually he devised his own method of getting just enough air. By means of a string and a series of hooks inserted at intervals into the upper half of the Dutch door he could obtain as little or as much air as he chose. It was not necessary to open a window or remove the sacking beneath the door or dig out the putty with which he had sealed the various cracks and crevices in the walls. As for the bloody lamps, he decided that he would use candles instead. The candles gave his cell a mortuary look which suited his morbid state of mind.

Meanwhile the itch continued to plague him. Every time he came down for meals he rolled up his sleeves or the legs of his trousers to show us the ravages it had made. His flesh was by now a mass of running sores. Had I been in his boots I would have put a bullet through my brain.

53

Obviously something had to be done or we would all go crazy. We had tried all the old-fashioned remedies—to no avail. In desperation I begged a friend who lived some few hundred miles away to make a special trip. He was a capable all-round physician, a surgeon and a psychiatrist to boot. He also knew some French. In fact, he was an altogether unusual fellow, and generous and frank. I knew that he would give me good advice if he could not cope with the case.

Well, he came. He examined Moricand from head to toe and inside out. That done, he engaged him in talk. He paid no further heed to the running sores, made no further mention of the subject. He talked about all manner of things but not about the itch. It was as if he had completely forgotten what he had been summoned for. Now and then Moricand attempted to remind him of the object of his visit but my friend always succeeded in diverting his attention to some other subject. Finally he made ready to leave, after writing out a prescription which he left under Moricand's nose.

I escorted him to the car, eager to know what he really thought.

"There's nothing to do," he said. "When he stops thinking about it the itch will disappear."

"And in the meantime. . . ?"

"Let him take the pills."

"Will they really help?"

"That depends on *him*. There's nothing in them to hurt him, or to do him any good. Unless he believes so."

There was a heavy pause.

Suddenly he said: "Do you want my honest advice?"

"I certainly do," said I.

"Then get him off your hands!"

"What do you mean?"

"Just that. You might as well have a leper living with you."

I must have looked sorely puzzled.

"It's simple," he said. "He doesn't want to get well. What he wants is sympathy, attention. He's not a man, he's a child. A spoiled child."

54

Another pause.

"And don't worry if he threatens to do himself in. He'll probably pull that on you when everything else fails. He won't kill himself. He loves himself too much."

"I see," said I. "So that's how it stands. . . . But what in hell will I tell him?"

"That I leave to you, old pal." He started up the motor.

"OK," I said. "Maybe I'll take the pills myself. Anyway, a thousand thanks!"

Moricand was lying in wait for me. He had been studying the prescription but could make nothing of it, the handwriting was too abominable.

In a few words I explained that in my friend's opinion his ailment was psychological.

"Any fool knows that!" he blurted out and in the next breath—"Is he really a doctor?"

"A quite famous one," I answered.

"Strange," said Moricand. "He talked like an imbecile. "OH?"

"Asking me if I still masturbated."

"*Et puis. . .?*"

"If I liked women as much as men. If I had ever taken drugs. If I believed in emanations. If, if, if. . . *C'est un fou!*"

For a minute or two he was speechless with rage. Then, in a tone of utter misery, he muttered as if to himself: "*Mon Dieu, mon Dieu, qu'est-ce que je peux faire? Comme je suis seul, tout seul!*"

"Come, come," I murmured, "calm yourself! There are worse things than the itch."

"*Like what?*" he demanded. He said it with such swiftness that I was taken aback.

"*Like what?*" he repeated. "*Psychological . . . pouah!* He must take me for an idiot. What a country this is! No humanity. No understanding. No intelligence. Ah, if only I could die . . . die tonight!"

I said not a word.

55

"May you never suffer, *mon cher Miller*, as I am suffering! The war was nothing compared to this."

Suddenly his glance fell on the prescription. He picked it up, clenched it in his fist, then threw it on the floor.

"*Pills!* He gives *me*, Moricand, pills! Bah!" He spat on the floor.

"He's a quack, your friend. A charlatan. An impostor."

Thus ended the first attempt to pull him out of his misery.

A week passed and then someone who should turn up but my old friend Gilbert. Ah, I thought, at last someone who speaks French, someone who loves French literature. What a treat for Moricand!

Over a bottle of wine I had no difficulty in getting them to talk to one another. It was only a matter of a few minutes before they were discussing Baudelaire, Villon, Voltaire, Gide, Cocteau, *les ballets russes, Ubu Roi*, and so forth. When I saw that they were hitting it off nicely I discreetly withdrew, hoping that Gilbert who had also suffered the afflictions of Job, would raise the other's morale. Or at least get him drunk.

An hour or so later, as I was sauntering down the road with the dog, Gilbert drove up.

"What, going so soon?" I said. It was unlike Gilbert to leave before the last bottle had been emptied.

"I've had a bellyful," he replied. "What a prick!"

"Who, Moricand?"

"Exactly."

"What happened?"

By way of answer he gave me a look of sheer disgust.

"Do you know what I'd do with him, *amigo?*" he said vengefully.

"No, what?"

"Push him over the cliff."

"That's easier said than done."

"Try it! It's the best solution." With that he stepped on the gas. Gilbert's words gave me a shock. It was altogether unlike him to talk that way about another person. He was such a kind, gentle, considerate soul, had been through such hell himself. Obviously it hadn't taken long for him to see through Moricand.

Meanwhile my good friend Lilik, who had rented a shack a few miles down the road, was doing his utmost to make Moricand more at home. Moricand liked Lilik and had implicit faith in him. He could hardly feel otherwise, since Lilik did nothing but render him services. Lilik would sit with him by the hour, listening to his tales of woe.

From Lilik I gleaned that Moricand thought I was not paying him enough attention. "You never inquire about his work," he said.

"His work? What work? What is he working at?"

"I believe he's writing his memoirs."

"That's interesting," I said. "I must have a look some time."

"By the way," said Lilik, "have you ever seen his drawings?"

"What drawings?"

"My God, haven't you seen them yet? He's got a whole stack of them in his portfolio. Erotic drawings. Lucky for you," he chuckled, "that the customs men didn't discover them."

"Are they any good?"

"Yes and no. They're certainly not for children to look at."

A few days after this conversation took place, an old friend turned up. Leon Shamroy. As usual, he was loaded with gifts. Mostly things to eat and drink.

This time Moricand opened his falcon eyes even wider.

"It's staggering," he murmured. He drew me to one side. "A millionaire, I suppose?"

"No, just the head camera man for the Fox Films. The man who wins all the Oscars."

"I only wish you could understand his talk," I added. "There's no one in all America who can say the things he says and get away with it."

Just then Leon broke in. "What's all the whispering about?" he demanded. "Who is this guy—one of your Montparnasse friends?

Doesn't he talk English? What's he doing here? Sponging on you, I'll bet. Give him a drink! He looks bored—or sad."

"Here, let him try one of these," said Leon, fishing a handful of cigars out of his breast pocket. "They only cost a dollar apiece. Maybe he'll get a kick out of them."

He nodded to Moricand to indicate that the cigars were for him. With that he threw away the half-finished Havana he had allowed to go out and lit a fresh one. The cigars were almost a foot long and thick as seven-year-old rattlers. They had a beautiful aroma too. Cheap at twice the price, thought I to myself.

"Tell him I don't talk French," said Leon, slightly annoyed because Moricand had expressed his thanks in long-winded French. As he spoke he undid a package out of which spilled some luscious-looking cheeses, some salami and some *lachs*. Over his shoulder: "Tell him we like to eat and drink. We'll chew the rag later. Hey, where's that wine I brought? No, wait a minute. I've got a bottle of Haig and Haig in the car. Let's give him that. The poor bugger, I'll bet he's never had a tumbler of whisky in his life. . . . Listen, what's the matter with him? Doesn't he ever crack a smile?"

He went on sputtering like that, opening more parcels, cutting himself a hunk of corn bread, buttering it with delicious sweet butter, spearing an olive, tasting an anchovy, then a sour pickle, a little of this, a little of that, at the same time unearthing a box of sweets for Val, together with a beautiful dress, a string of beads and . . . *"Here,* this is for *you,* you bastard!" and he flung me a tin. of expensive cigarettes. "I've got more for you up in the car. By the way, I forgot to ask you—how are things going with you? Haven't made your pile yet, have you? You and Bufano! A couple of orphans. Lucky you have a friend like me . . . someone who *works* for a living, what?"

Meanwhile Lilik had gone to the car and brought things down. We opened the Haig and Haig, then a beautiful brand of Bordeaux for Moricand (and for ourselves), looked appraisingly at the

Pernod and the Chartreuse which he had also thought to bring. The air was already thick with smoke, the floor littered with paper and string.

"Is that shower of yours still working?" asked Leon, unbuttoning his silk shirt. "I've got to take one soon. Haven't had any sleep for thirty-six hours. Christ, am I glad to get away for a few hours! By the way, can you bunk me for the night? Maybe two nights? I want to talk to you. We've got to make some real dough for you soon. You don't want to be a beggar all your life, do you? Don't answer! I know what you're going to say. . . . By the way, where are your water colors? Drag 'em out! You know me, I may buy a half dozen before I leave. If they're any good, I mean."

Suddenly he noticed Moricand was pulling on a cheroot.

"What's the matter with that guy?" he shouted. "What's he got that stink weed in his mouth for? Didn't we just give him some good cigars?"

Moricand explained blushingly that he was reserving the cigars for later. They were too good to smoke immediately. He wanted to fondle them a while before lighting up.

"Fuck that nonsense!" cried Leon. "Tell him he's in America now. We don't worry about tomorrow, do we? Tell him when he finishes those I'll send him a box from L.A." He turned his head away, lowered his voice a trifle, "What's griping him anyway? Has he been starved to death over there? Anyway, the hell with him! Look, I want to tell you a little joke I heard the other night. Translate it for him, will you? I want to see if he'll laugh."

My wife is making a vain attempt to set the table. Leon has already embarked on his little joke, a filthy one, and Lilik is farting like a stallion. In the middle of his tale Leon pauses to cut himself another hunk of bread, pour a drink, take off his shoes and socks, spear an olive, and so on. Moricand watches him goggle-eyed. A new specimen of humanity for him. *Le vrai type américain, quoi!* I have a suspicion he's really enjoying himself. Sampling the Bordeaux, he smacks his lips. The *lachs*

59

intrigues him. As for the corn bread, he's never seen or tasted it before. Famous! *Ausgezeichnet!*

Lilik's laughing so hard the tears are rolling down his cheeks. It's a good joke, and a filthy one, but difficult to translate.

"What's the trouble?" says Leon. "Don't they use that kind of language where he comes from?"

He observes Moricand diving into the viands, sipping his wine, trying to puff away at the huge Havana.

"O.K. Forget the joke! He's filling his belly, that's good enough. Listen, what did you say he was again?"

"Among other things an astrologer," I said.

"He doesn't know his ass from a hole in the ground. *Astrology!* Who wants to listen to that shit? Tell him to get wise to himself. . . . Hey, wait a minute, Ill give him my birth date. Let's see what he makes of it."

I give the dope to Moricand. He says he's not ready yet. Wants to observe Leon a little longer, if we don't mind.

"What did he say?"

"He says he wants to enjoy his food first. But he knows that you're an exceptional type." I added this to relieve the tension.

"He said a mouthful there. You're damned right I'm an exceptional type. Anyone else in my place would go crazy. Tell him for me that I've got his number, will you?" Then, turning directly to Moricand, he says: "How's the wine . . . the *vin rouge?* Good stuff, what?"

"*Epatant!*" says Moricand, unaware of all the innuendos that had passed under his nose.

"You bet your ass it's good," says Leon. "I bought it. I know good stuff when I see it."

He watches Moricand as if his nibs were a trained otter, then turns to me. "Does he do anything else beside read the stars?" Giving me a reproachful look, he adds: "I'll bet he likes nothing better than to sit on his fat fanny all day. Why don't you put him to work? Get him to dig a garden, plant vegetables, hoe the

60

weeds. That's what he needs. I know these bastards. They're all alike."

My wife was getting uncomfortable. She didn't want Moricand's feelings to be hurt.

"He's got something in his room you'll enjoy seeing," she said to Leon.

"Yeah," said Lilik, "right up your street, Leon."

"What are you trying to pull on me? What's the big secret? Out with it!"

We explained. Leon seemed strangely disinterested.

"Hollywood's full of that crap," he said. "What do you want me to do—*masturbate?*"

The afternoon wore on. Moricand retired to his cell. Leon took us up to inspect his new car, which could do ninety per in nothing flat. Suddenly he remembered that he had some toys for Val in the back of the car. "Where's Bufano these days?" says he, fishing around in the trunk.

"Gone to India, I think."

"To see Nehru, I bet!" He chuckled. "How that guy gets around without a cent in his pockets beats me. By the way, what are *you* doing for money these days?"

With this he dives into his pants pocket, hauls out a wad of greenbacks fastened with a clip, and begins peeling off a few.

"Here, take this," he says, shoving the greenbacks in my fist. "I'll probably owe you money before I leave."

"Have you anything good to read?" he asks suddenly. "Like that Giono book you lent me, remember? What about that guy Cendrars you're always pissing in the pants about? Has any of his stuff been translated yet?" He threw another half-finished Havana away, crushed it under his heel, and lit a fresh one. "I suppose you think I never look at a book. You're wrong. I read plenty. . . . Some day you're going to write a script for me—and earn some real dough. By the way"—he jerked his thumb in the

61

direction of Moricand's studio—"is that guy taking you for a lot of dough? You're a chump. How did you ever fall into the trap?"

I told him it was a long story . . . some other time.

"What about those drawings of his? Should I have a look? He wants to sell them, I suppose? I wouldn't mind taking some—if it would help *you* out. . . . Wait a minute, I want to take a crap first."

When he returned he had a fresh cigar in his mouth. He was looking roseate.

"There's nothing like a good crap," he said, beaming. "Now let's visit that sad-looking bimbo. And fetch Lilik, will you? I want his opinion before I let myself in for anything."

As we entered Moricand's cell Leon sniffed the air. "For Christ's sake, make him open a window!" he exclaimed.

"Can't, Leon. He's afraid of draughts."

"Just like him, for crying out loud. O.K. Tell him to trot his dirty pictures out—and make it snappy, eh? I'll puke up if we have to stay here more than ten minutes."

Moricand proceeded to get out his handsome leather portfolio. He placed it circumspectly before him, then calmly lit a *gauloise bleue*.

"Ask him to put it out," begged Leon. He drew a pack of Chesterfields from his pocket and offered Moricand one. Moricand politely refused, saying he couldn't stand American cigarettes.

"He's nuts!" said Leon. *"Here!"* and he proffered Moricand a big cigar.

Moricand declined the offer. "I like these better," he said, brandishing his foul French cigarette.

"If that's how it is, fuck it!" said Leon. "Tell him to get going. We can't waste the whole afternoon in this tomb."

But Moricand wasn't to be hurried. He had his own peculiar way of presenting his work. He allowed no one to touch the drawings. He held them in front of him, turning them slowly, page by page, as if they were ancient papyri to be handled with a shovel only. Now and then he drew a silk handkerchief from his breast pocket to remove the perspiration from his hands.

It was my first view of his work. I must confess the drawings left a bad taste in my mouth. They were perverse, sadistic, sacrilegious. Children being raped by lubricious monsters, virgins practicing all manner of illicit intercourse, nuns defiling themselves with sacred objects . . . flagellations, medieval tortures, dismemberments, coprophagic orgies, and so forth. All done with a delicate, sensitive hand, which only magnified the disgusting element of the subject matter.

For once Leon was nonplused. He turned to Lilik inquiringly. Asked to see some of them a second time.

"The bugger knows how to draw, doesn't he?" he remarked.

Lilik hereupon pointed out a few he thought were exceptionally well executed.

"I'll take them," said Leon. "How much?"

Moricand named a price. A stiff one, even for an American client.

"Tell him to wrap them up," said Leon. "They're not worth it, but I'll take them. I know someone would give his right arm to own one."

He fished out his wad, counted the bills rapidly, and shoved them back into his pocket.

"Can't spare the cash," he said. "Tell him I'll send him a check when I get home . . . *if he'll trust me.*"

At this point Moricand seemed to undergo a change of heart. Said he didn't want to sell them singly. All or nothing. He named a price for the lot. A whopping price.

"He's mad," shrieked Leon. "Let him stick 'em up his ass!"

I explained to Moricand that Leon would have to think it over.

"Okay," said Moricand, giving me a wry, knowing smile. I knew that in *his* mind the bird was in the bag. A handful of trumps, that's what he was holding. "Okay," he repeated as we took leave of him.

63

As we sauntered down the steps Leon blurted out: "If the bastard had any brains he'd offer to let me take the portfolio and show them around. I could probably get twice what he's asking. They might get soiled, of course. What a finicky prick!" He gave me a sharp nudge. "That'd be something, wouldn't it, *to dirty that smut!*"

At the foot of the steps he paused a moment and caught me by the arm.

"You know what's the matter with him? He's *sick*." He touched his cranium with his forefinger.

"When you get rid of him," he added, "you'd better disinfect the place."

Some few nights later, at the dinner table, we at last drifted into the subject of the war. Moricand was in excellent form and only too eager to relate his experiences. Why we had never touched on all this before I don't know. To be sure, in his letters from Switzerland he had given me an outline of all that had taken place since we parted that night in June of 1939. But I had forgotten most of it. I knew that he had joined the Foreign Legion, for the second time, joined it not out of patriotism but to survive. How else was he to obtain food and shelter? He lasted only a few months in the Legion, of course, being altogether unfit for the rigors of that life. Discharged, he had returned to his garret in the Hotel Modial, more desperate, naturally, than ever before. He was in Paris when the Germans marched in. The presence of the Germans didn't bother him as much as the absence of food. At the last ditch he ran into an old friend, a man who held an important post at Radio-Paris. The friend took him on. It meant money, food, cigarettes. An odious job, but. . . . At any rate, the friend was now in prison. A collaborator, evidently.

He rehearsed the whole period again, this evening, and in great detail. As though he felt compelled to get it off his chest. From time to time I lost the thread. Never interested in politics, in feuds,

64

in intrigues and rivalries, I became utterly confused just at the crucial period when, by command of the Germans, he intimated that he had been forced to go to Germany. (They had even picked out a wife for him to marry.) Suddenly the whole picture got out of whack. I lost him in a vacant lot with a Gestapo agent holding a revolver against his spine. It was all an absurd and horrendous nightmare anyway. Whether he had been in the service of the Germans or not—he never defined his position clearly—was all one to me. I wouldn't have minded if he had quietly informed me that he had turned traitor. What I *was* curious about was—how did he manage to get out of the mess? How did it happen that he came off with a whole skin?

Of a sudden I realize that he's telling me of his escape. We're no longer in Germany, but in France . . . or is it Belgium or Luxembourg? He's headed for the Swiss border. Bogged down by two heavy valises which he's been dragging for days and weeks. One day he's between the French Army and the German Army, the next day between the American Army and the German Army. Sometimes its neutral terrain he's traversing, sometimes it's no mans land. Wherever he goes it's the same story: no food, no shelter, no aid. He has to get ill to obtain a little nourishment, a place to flop, and so forth. Finally he really is ill. With a valise in each hand he marches on from place to place, shaking with fever, parched with thirst, dizzy, dopey, desperate. Above the cannonade he can hear his empty guts rattling. The bullets whizz overhead, the stinking dead lie in heaps everywhere, the hospitals are over-crowded, the fruit trees bare, the houses demolishd, the roads filled with homeless, sick, crippled, wounded, forlorn, abandoned souls. Every man for himself! War! War! And there he is floundering around in the midst of it: a Swiss neutral with a passport and an empty belly. Now and then an American soldier flings him a cigarette. But no Yardley's talc. No toilet paper. No perfumed soap. And with it all he's got the itch. Not only the itch, but lice. Not only lice, but scurvy.

The armies, all sixty-nine of them, are battling it out around him. They don't seem to care at all for his safety. But the war is definitely coming to an end. It's all over but the mopping up. Nobody knows why he's fighting, nor for whom. The Germans are licked but they won't surrender. Idiots. Bloody idiots. In fact, everybody's licked except the Americans. They, the goofy Americans, are romping through in grand style, their kits crammed with tasty snacks, their pockets loaded with cigarettes, chewing gum, flasks, crap-shooting dice and what not. The highest paid warriors that ever donned uniform. Money to burn and nothing to spend it on. Just praying to get to Paris, praying for a chance to rape the lascivious French girls—or old hags, if there are no girls left. And as they romp along they burn their garbage—while starving civilians watch in horror and stupefaction. *Orders.* Keep moving! Keep liquidating! On, on . . . on to Paris! On to Berlin! On to Moscow! Swipe what you can, guzzle what you can, rape what you can. And if you can't, shit on it! But don't beef! Keep going, keep moving, keep advancing! The end is near. Victory is in sight. Up with the flag! Hourrah! Hourrah! And fuck the generals, fuck the admirals! Fuck your way through! Now or never! What a grand time! What a lousy mess! What horripilating insanity!

("I am that General So-and-So who is responsible for the death of so many of your beloved!")

Like a ghost our dear Moricand, by now witless and shitless, is running the gauntlet, moving like a frantic rat between the opposing armies, skirting them, flanking them, outwitting them, running head on into them; in his fright speaking good English now and then, or German, or just plain horseshit, anything to disengage himself, anything to wiggle free, but always clinging to his saddlebags which now weigh a ton, always headed for the Swiss border, despite detours, loops, hairpin turns, double-eagles, sometimes crawling on all fours, sometimes walking erect, sometimes smothered under a load of manure, sometimes doing the St. Vitus dance.

Always going forward, unless pushed backward. Finally reaching the border, only to find that it is blocked. Retracing his steps. Back to the starting point. Double fire. Diarrhea. Fever and more fever. Cross-examinations. Vaccinations. Evacuations. New armies to contend with. New battle fronts. New bulges. New victories. New retreats. And more dead and wounded, naturally. More vultures. More unfragrant breezes.

Yet always and anon he manages to hold on to his Swiss passport, his two valises, his slender sanity, his desperate hope of freedom.

"And what was in those valises that made them so precious?"

"Everything I cherish," he answered.

"Like what?"

"My books, my diaries, my writings, my. . . ."

I looked at him flabbergasted.

"No, Christ! You don't mean to say. . . ."

"Yes," he said, "just books, papers, horoscopes, excerpts from Plotinus, Iamblichus, Claude Saint-Martin. . . ."

I couldn't help it, I began to laugh. I laughed and laughed and laughed. I thought I'd never stop laughing.

He was offended. I apologized.

"You lugged all that crap around like an elephant," I exclaimed, "at the risk of losing your own hide?"

"A man doesn't throw away everything that is precious to him —just like that!"

"I would!" I exclaimed.

"But my whole life was bound up in those encumbrances."

"You should have thrown your life away too!"

"Not Moricand!" he replied, and his eyes flashed fire.

Suddenly I no longer felt sorry for him, not for anything that had ever happened to him.

For days those two valises weighed me down. They weighed as heavily on my mind and spirit as they had on Moricand's when he was crawling like a bedbug over that crazy quilt called Europe. I dreamed about them too. Sometimes he appeared in a dream,

Moriand, looking like Emil Jannings, the Jannings of *The Last Laugh*, the Grand Hotel porter Jannings, who has been sacked, who has lost his standing, who furtively smuggles his uniform out each night after he has been demoted to attendant in the toilet and washroom. In my dreams I was forever shadowing poor Conrad, always within shouting distance of him yet never able to make him hear me, what with the cannonades, the blitz bombs, the machine-gun fire, the screams of the wounded, the shrieks of the dying. Everywhere war and desolation. Here a shell crater filled with arms and legs; here a warrior still warm, his buttons ripped off, his proud genitals missing; here a freshly bleached skull crawling with bright red worms; a child impaled on a fence post; a gun carriage reeking with blood and vomit; trees standing upside down, dangling with human limbs, an arm to which a hand is still attached, the remains of a hand buried in a glove. Or animals in stampede, their eyes blazing with insanity, their legs a blur, their hides aflame, their bowels hanging out, tripping them, and behind them thousands more, millions of them, all singed, scorched, racked, torn, battered, bleeding, vomiting, racing like mad, racing ahead of the dead, racing for the Jordan, shorn of all medals, passports, halters, bits, bridles, feathers, fur, bills and hollyhocks. And Conrad Moriturus ever ahead, fleeing, his feet shod in patent leather boots, his hair neatly pomaded, his nails manicured, his linen starched, his mustache waxed, his trousers pressed. Galloping on like the Flying Dutchman, his valises swinging like ballast, his cold breath congealing behind him like frozen vapor. *To the border! To the border!*

And that was Europe! A Europe I never saw, a Europe I never tasted. Ah, Iamblichus, Porphyry, Erasmus, Duns Scotus, where are we? What elixir are we drinking? What wisdom are we sucking? Define the alphabet, O wise ones! Measure the itch! Flog insanity to death, if you can! Are those stars looking down upon us, or are they burnt holes in a filament of sick flesh? And where is General Doppelgänger now, and General Eisenhower, and General Pussyfoot Cornelius Triphammer? Where the enemy? Where is Jack and where is Jill? How I would like to put a message through—to the Divine Creator! But I can't remember the name. I'm so utterly harmless, so innocent. Just a neutral. Nothing to declare but two valises. Yes, a citizen. A quiet sort of madman, nothing more. I ask for no decorations, no monuments in my name. Just see that the bags get through. I'll follow afterwards. I'll be there, even if I'm only a trunk. Moriturus, that's my name. Swiss, yes. A *légionnaire. Un mutilé de la guerre.* Call me anything you like. *Iamblichus,* if you wish. Or just— "The Itch"!

Taking advantage of the rainy season, we decided to break ground for a vegetable patch. We chose a spot that had never been dug up before. I began with a pick and my wife continued with the spade. I suppose Moricand felt slightly conscience-stricken to see a woman doing such work. To our surprise, he offered to do some spading himself. After a half-hour he was all in. It made him feel good just the same. In fact, he felt so good that after lunch he asked if we would put on some phonograph records—he was dying to listen to a little music. As he listened he hummed and whistled. He asked if we had any of Grieg's music, *Peer Gynt* particularly. Said he used to play the piano long ago. Played by ear. Then he added that he thought Grieg was a very great composer; he liked him best of all. That knocked me for a loop.

My wife had put on a Viennese waltz. Now he really became animated. All of a sudden he went up to my wife and asked her if she would dance with him. I nearly fell off the chair. Moricand dancing! It seemed incredible. Preposterous. But he did, and with heart and soul. He whirled and whirled around until he got dizzy.

"You dance beautifully," said my wife, as he took a seat, panting and perspiring.

"You're still a young man," I threw in.

"I haven't done this since the year 1920 something," he said almost

69

blushingly. He slapped his thigh. "It's an old carcass but it still has a bit of life."

"Would you like to hear Harry Lauder?" I asked.

For a moment he was perplexed. Lauder, Lauder. . .? Then he got it.

"Certainly," he said. Obviously he was in a mood to hear anything.

I put on "Roamin' in the Gloamin'." To my amazement he even tried to sing. I thought perhaps he had had a little too much wine at lunch, but no, it wasn't the wine or the food this time, he was just happy for once.

The horrible thing is that it was almost more pitiful to see him happy than sad.

In the midst of these pleasantries Jean Wharton walked in. She was living just above us now in a house which she had recently had built. She had met Moricand once or twice before, but merely to exchange greetings. This day, being in extraordinary good humor, he mustered enough English to carry on a little conversation with her. When she left he remarked that she was a very interesting woman, rather attractive too. He added that she had a magnetic personality, that she radiated health and joy. He thought it might be well to cultivate her acquaintance, she made him feel good.

He felt so good, indeed, that he brought his memoirs down for me to read.

All in all, it was a remarkable day for Moricand. The best day of all, however, was the day Jaime de Angulo came down from his mountain top to pay us a visit. He came expressly to meet Moricand. We had, of course, informed Moricand of Jaime's existence, but we had never made a point of bringing the two together. To tell the truth, I didn't think they would get along very well together, since they seemed to have so little in common. Besides, I was never certain how Jaime would behave after he had a few drinks under his belt. The occasions when he did visit us and leave

70

without making a scene, without cursing, reviling and insulting everyone, were few and far between.

It was shortly after lunch that Jaime rode up, hitched his horse to the oak tree, gave it a punch in the ribs, and descended the steps. It was a bright, sunny day, rather warm for a day in February. As usual, Jaime wore a bright headband around his forehead—his dirty snotrag, probably. Brown as a walnut, gaunt, slightly bow-legged, he was still handsome, still very much the Spaniard—and still utterly unpredictable. With a feather in his headband, a little grease paint, a different costume, he might have passed for a Chip-pewa or a Shawnee Indian. He was definitely the outlaw.

As they greeted one another I could not help but remark the contrast they presented, these two figures (born only five days apart) who had passed their youth in a sedate, aristocratic quarter of Paris. Two "Little Lord Fauntleroys" who had seen the seamy side of life, whose days were now numbered, and who would never meet again. The one neat, orderly, immaculate, fussy, cautious, a man of the city, a recluse, a stargazer; the other the exact opposite. The one a pedestrian, the other a cavalier. The one an aesthete, the other a wild duck.

I was wrong in thinking they had so little in common. They had much in common. Aside from a common culture, a common language, a common background, a common love of books, librar-ies, research, a common gift of speech, a common addiction—the one to drugs, the other to alcohol—they had an even greater tie: their obsession with evil. Jaime was one of the very few men I ever met of whom I could say that he had a streak of the Devil in him. As for Moricand, he had always been a diabolist. The only differ-ence in their attitude toward the Devil was that Moricand feared him and Jaime cultivated him. At least, it always seemed thus to me. Both were confirmed atheists and thoroughly anti-Christian. Moricand leaned toward the antique pagan world, Jaime toward the primitive. Both were what we would call men of culture, men of learning, men of elegance. Jaime, playing the savage or the sot,

71

was still a man of exquisite taste; no matter how much he spat on all that was "refined," he never truly outgrew the Little Lord Fauntleroy he had been as a boy. It was only through dire necessity that Moricand had renounced *la vie mondaine*; at heart he remained the dandy, the fop, the snob.

When I brought out the bottle and the glasses—the bottle only half-full, by the way—I anticipated trouble. It did not seem possible that these two individuals, having traveled such divergent paths, could get along together for long.

I was wrong about everything this day. They not only got along, they scarcely touched the wine. They were intoxicated with something stronger than wine—the past.

The mention of the Avenue Henri-Martin—they had discovered in the space of a few minutes that they had been raised in the very same block!—started the ball rolling. Dwelling on his boyhood, Jaime at once began to mimic his parents, impersonate his schoolmates, re-enact his devilries, switching from French to Spanish and back again, acting now as a sissy, now as a coy young female, now as an irate Spanish grandee, now as a petulant, doting mother. Moricand was in stitches. Never did I believe that he could laugh so hard or so long. He was no longer the melancholy grampus, nor even the wise old owl, but a normal, natural human being who was enjoying himself.

Not to intrude on this festival of reminiscence, I threw myself on the bed in the middle of the room and pretended to take a nap.

But my ears were wide open.

In the space of a few short hours it seemed to me that Jaime succeeded in rehearsing the whole of his tumultuous life. And what a life it was! From Passy to the Wild West—in one jump. From being the son of a Spanish grandee, raised in the lap of luxury, to becoming a cowboy, a doctor of medicine, an anthropologist, a master of linguistics, and finally a cattle rancher on the crest of the Santa Lucia range here in Big Sur. A lone wolf, divorced from all he held dear, waging a perpetual feud with his neighbor Boronda, another Spaniard, poring over his books, his dictionaries (Chinese, Sanskrit, Hebrew, Arabic, Persian, to mention but a few), raising a little fruit and vegetables, killing deer in season and out, forever exercising his horses, getting drunk, quarreling with everyone, even his bosom pals, driving visitors away with the lash, studying in the dead of night, coming back to his book on language, *the* book on language, he hoped it would be!—and finishing it just before his death.... Between times twice married, three children, one of them his beloved son, crushed to death beneath him in a mysterious automobile accident, a tragedy which had a lasting effect upon him.

Odd to listen to it all from the bed. Strange to hear the so-called shaman talking to the sage, the anthropologist to the astrologer, the scholar to the scholar, the linguist to the bookworm, the horseman to the boulevardier, the adventurer to the hermit, the barbarian to the dandy, the lover of languages to the lover of words, the scientist to the occultist, the desperado to the ex-*Légionnaire*, the fiery Spaniard to the stolid Swiss, the uncouth native to the well-dressed gentleman, the anarchist to the civilized European, the rebel to the well-behaved citizen, the man of the open spaces to the man of the garret, the drunkard to the dope fiend....

Every quarter hour the *pendule* gave out its melodious chimes. Finally I hear them speaking soberly, earnestly, as if it were a matter of grave concern. It is about language. Moricand says but little now. He is all ears. With all his knowledge, I suspect that he never dreamed that on this North American continent there once were spoken so many varieties of tongues, languages, not dialects merely, languages great and small, obscure and rudimentary, some extremely complicated, baroque, one might say, in form and structure. How could he know—few Americans know—that side by side there existed tribes whose languages were as far apart as is Bantu from Sanskrit, or Finnish from Phoenician, or Basque from German. The idea had never entered his head, cosmopolite that he was, that in a remote corner of the globe known as Big Sur a man named Jaime de Angulo, a renegade and a reprobate, was spending his days and nights comparing, classifying, analyzing, dissecting roots, declensions, prefixes and suffixes, etymologies, homologies, affinities and anomalies of tongues and dialects borrowed from all continents, all times, all races and conditions of man. Never had he thought it possible to combine in one person, as did this Angulo, the savage, the scholar, the man of the world, the recluse, the idealist and the very son of Lucifer. Well might he say, as he did later: *"C'est un être formidable. C'est un homme, celui-là!"*

Yes, he was indeed that, *a man*, dear Jaime de Angulo! A beloved, hated, detested, endearing, charming, cantankerous, pesky, devil-worshiping son-of-a-bitch of a man with a proud heart and a defiant soul, filled with tenderness and compassion for all humanity, yet cruel, vicious, mean and ornery. His own worst enemy. A man doomed to end his days in horrible agony—mutilated, emasculated, humiliated to the very core of his being. Yet even unto the end preserving his reason, his lucidity, his devil-may-care spirit, his defiance of God and man—and his great impersonal ego.

Would they ever have become bosom friends? I doubt it. Fortunate it was that Moricand never carried out his resolution to walk to the top of the mountain and offer a hand in friendship. Despite all they had in common they were worlds apart. Not even the Devil himself could have united them in friendship and brotherhood.

Reviewing their encounter that afternoon in my mind's eye, **I see them as two egomaniacs hypnotized for a few brief hours by the mingling of worlds which overshadowed their personalities, their interests, their philosophies of life.**

There are conjunctions in the human sphere which are just as fleeting and mysterious as stellar ones, conjunctions which seem like violation of natural law. For me who observed the event, it was like witnessing the marriage of fire and water.

Now that they have both passed beyond, one may be pardoned

74

for wondering if they will ever meet again, and in what realm. They had so much to undo, so much to discover, so much to live out! Such lonely souls, full of pride, full of knowledge, full of the world and its evils! Not a grain of faith in either of them. Hugging the world and reviling it; clinging to life and desecrating it; fleeing society and never coming face to face with God; playing the mage and the shaman, but never acquiring wisdom of life or the wisdom of love. In what realm, I ask myself, will they meet again? And will they recognize one another?

One bright day as I was passing Moricand's cell—I had just dumped some garbage over the cliff—I found him leaning over the lower half of the Dutch door as if in contemplation. I was in an excellent mood because, as always when dumping the garbage, I had been rewarded by a breath-taking view of the coast. This particular morning everything was bright and still; the sky, the water, the mountains stared back at me as if reflected in a mirror. If the earth weren't curved I could have gazed right into China, the atmosphere was that clean and clear.

"*Il fait beau aujourd'hui*," said I, depositing the garbage can to light a cigarette.

"*Oui, il fait beau*," said he. "Come in a minute, won't you?"

I stepped in and took a seat beside his writing table. What now? I wondered. Another consultation?

He lit a cigarette slowly, as if debating how to begin. Had I been given ten thousand guesses, I could never have guessed what he was about to say. However, I was, as I say, in a most excellent mood; it mattered little to me what was disturbing him. My own mind was free, clear, empty.

"*Mon cher Miller*," he began in an even, steady tone, "what you are doing to me no man has a right to do to another."

I looked at him uncomprehendingly. "What I am doing to *you*...?"

"Yes," he said. "You don't realize perhaps what you've done."

75

I made no reply. I was too curious to know what would follow to feel even the least indignation.

"You invited me to come here, to make this my home for the rest of my days. . . . You said I did not need to work, that I could do anything I pleased. And you demanded nothing in return. One can't do that to a fellow-man. It's unjust. It puts me in an unbearable position." It was undermining, he wanted to say.

He paused a moment. I was too flabbergasted to make reply immediately.

"Besides," he continued, "this is no place for me. I am a man of the city; I miss the pavement under my feet. If there were only a café I could walk to, or a library, or a cinema. I'm a prisoner here." He looked around him. "This is where I spend my days—and nights. Alone. No one to talk to. Not even you. You're too busy most of the time. Moreover, I feel that you're uninterested in what I am doing. . . . What am I to do, sit here until I die? You know I am not a man to complain. I keep to myself as much as I can; I occupy myself with my work, I take a walk now and then, I read . . . and I scratch myself continually. How long can I put up with it? Some days I feel as if I will go mad. I don't belong. . . ."

"I think I understand you," said I. "It's too bad it worked out this way. I meant only to do you a good turn."

"Oui, je le sais, mon vieux! It's all my fault. Nevertheless. . . ."

"What would you have me do? Send you back to Paris? That's impossible—at least right now."

"I know that," he said.

What he didn't know was that I was still struggling to pay back what I had borrowed to bring him to America.

"I was just wondering," he said, drumming his fingers on the table top, "how a city like San Francisco might be."

"Very good for a while," I said, "but how manage it? There's nothing you could work at, and I certainly couldn't support you there."

76

"Of course not," he said, "I wouldn't think of it. My God, you've done plenty already. More than enough. I shall never be able to repay you."

"Let's not go into *that!* The point is that you're unhappy here. Nobody is to blame. How could either of us have foreseen such an issue? I'm glad you spoke your mind. Perhaps if we put our heads together we can find a solution. It's true that I haven't given you or your work much attention, but you see what my life is like. You know how little time I have for my own work. You know, I too would like to walk the streets of Paris once in a while, feel the pavement under my feet, as you say. I too would like to be able to go to a café when I feel like it and meet a few congenial spirits. Of course, I'm in a different position from you. I'm not miserable here. Never. No matter what happens. If I had plenty of money I would get up and travel, I would invite my old friends to come and stay with me.... "I'd do all sorts of things I don't even dream of now. But one thing is certain in my mind—that this is a paradise. If anything goes wrong, I most certainly will not attribute it to the place.... It's a beautiful day today, no? It will be beautiful tomorrow when it pours. It's beautiful too when the fog settles down over everything and blacks us out. It was beautiful to *you* when you first saw it. It will be beautiful when you have gone.... Do you know what's wrong? (I tapped my skull.) *This up here!* A day like today I realize what I've told you a hundred different times—that there's nothing wrong with the world. What's wrong is our way of looking at it."

He gave me a wan smile, as if to say, "Just like Miller to go off on such a tangent. I say I'm suffering and he says everything is perfect."

"I know what you're thinking," I said. "Believe me, I feel for you. But you must try to do something for yourself. I did the best I could; if I made a mistake, then you must help me. Legally I'm responsible for you; morally you are responsible only to yourself. Nobody can help you but yourself. You think that I am

77

indifferent to your suffering. You think I treat the itch too lightly, I don't. All I say is, find out what itches you. You can scratch and scratch, but unless you discover what's itching you you will never get relief."

"*C'est assez vrai*," he said. "I've reached bottom."

He hung his head a few moments, then looked up. An idea had flashed through his mind.

"Yes," he said, "I am that desperate that I am willing to try anything."

I was wondering what exactly that might mean when he promptly added: "This woman, Madame Wharton, what do you think of her?"

I smiled. It was a rather big question.

"I mean, does she really have healing powers?"

"Yes, she does," said I.

"Do you think she could help *me?*"

"That depends," I replied. "Depends greatly on you, on whether you want to be helped or not. You could cure yourself, I believe, if you had enough faith in yourself."

He ignored this last. Began pumping me about her views, her methods of operation, her background, and so on.

"I could tell you a great deal about her," I said. "I could talk to you all day, in fact. But what would it matter? If you wish to put yourself in someone else's hands, you must surrender completely. What she believes in is one thing; what she can do for you is another. If I were in your boots, if I were as desperate as you pretend to be, I wouldn't care how the trick was accomplished. All I would care about would be to get well."

He swallowed this as best he could, remarking that Moricand was not Miller and vice versa. He added that he believed her to be highly intelligent, though he confessed he could not always follow her thoughts. There was something of the mystic or the occult about her, he suspected.

"You're wrong there," I said. "She has no use for mysticism *or* occultism. If she believes in magic, it's everyday magic . . . such as Jesus practiced."

"I hope she doesn't want to convert me first," he sighed. "I have no patience with that humbug, you know."

"Maybe that's what you need," I said laughingly.

"*Non!* Seriously," he said, "do you think I could put myself in her hands? My God, even if it's Christianity she's going to spout, I'm willing to listen. I'll try *anything*. Anything to get rid of this horrible, horrible itch. I'll *pray*, if she wants me to."

"I don't think she'll ask you to do anything you don't want to do, my dear Moricand. She's not the sort to force her opinions on you. But I do think this. . . . If you listen to her seriously, if you believe that she can do something for you, you may find that you will think and act in different fashion than you now believe possible. Anyway, don't think one way and act another—not with *her!* She'll see through you immediately. And, after all, you wouldn't be fooling *her*, only yourself."

"Then she does have definite views . . . *religious* views, I mean?"

"Of course! That is, if you want to put it that way."

"What do you mean by that?" He looked slightly alarmed.

"I mean, old chap, that she has no religious views whatever. She's religious through and through. She acts out her views or beliefs. She doesn't think *about*, she thinks. She thinks things through—and acts them out. What she thinks about life, God, and all that, is very simple, so simple that you may not understand it at first. She's not a thinker, in *your* sense of the word. To her, Mind is all. What one thinks, one is. If there's something wrong with you, it's because your thinking is wrong. Does that make sense?"

"*C'est bien simple*," he said, nodding his head dolorously. (Too simple! is what he meant.) Obviously he would have been more excited had I made it sound intricate, abstruse, difficult to follow. Anything simple and direct was suspect to him. Besides, in his mind healing powers were magical powers, powers acquired through study, discipline, training, powers based on mastery over

79

secret processes. Furthest from his mind was the thought that any-one could enter into direct communication with the source of all power.

"There's a force in her," he said, "a vitality which is physical and which I know can be communicated. She may not know from where it derives, but she possesses it and radiates it. Some times ignorant people have these powers."

"She's not ignorant, I can tell you that!" I said. "And if it *is* a physical force you feel in her presence you will never capture it for yourself, unless. . . ."

"Unless what?" he exclaimed eagerly.

"I won't say now. I think we've talked enough about her. After all, no matter what I tell you, the result depends on *you*, not her. Nobody has ever been cured of anything who did not want to be cured. The converse is just as true, only it's more difficult to swal-low. It's always easier to take a negative view than a positive one. Anyway, whether the itch stops or not, it will be an interesting experiment for you. But think about it before you ask her aid. And you must ask her yourself, *compris?*"

"Don't worry," he replied. "I'll ask her. I'll ask her today, if I see her. I don't care what she orders me to do. I'll get down on my knees and pray, if that's what she wants. Anything! I'm at my wit's end."

"Good!" said I. *"On verra."*

It was too wonderful a morning to surrender myself to the ma-chine. I took myself to the forest, alone, and when I had come to the usual halting place beside the pool, I sat down on a log, put my head in my hands and began to laugh. I laughed at myself, then at him, then at fate, then at the wild waves going up and down, because my head was full of nothing but wild waves going up and down. All in all, it was a lucky break. Fortunately, we were not married to one another; there were no children, no compli-cations. Even if he wanted to return to Paris, I believed I could manage it somehow. That is, with a little cooperation on his part. But what a lesson he had given me! Never, never again, would

I make the mistake of trying to solve someone's problems for him. How deceptive to think that by means of a little self-sacrifice one can help another overcome his difficulties! How egotistical! And how right he was to say that I had undermined him! Right and yet wrong! Because, making a reproach like that, he should have followed it up with—"I'm leaving. Leaving tomorrow. And this time I won't even take a toothbrush with me. I'll strike out on my own, come what may. The worst that can happen to me is to be deported. Even if they ship me back to Hell it's better than being a burden to someone. At least, I'll be able to scratch myself in peace!"

At this point I thought of a strange thing—that I too was suffering from the itch, only it was an itch one couldn't get at, an itch that didn't manifest itself bodily. But it was there just the same . . . there where every itch begins and ends. The unfortunate part about my ailment was that nobody ever caught me scratching. Yet I was at it night and day, feverishly, frantically, without let. Like Paul, I was constantly saying to myself: "Who shall deliver me from the body of this death?" What irony that people should be writing me from all over the world, thanking me for the encouragement and inspiration my work had given them. No doubt they looked upon me as an emancipated being. Yet every day of my life I was fighting a corpse, a ghost, a cancer that had taken possession of my mind and that ravaged me more than any bodily affliction possibly could. Every day I had to meet and battle anew with the person I had chosen as a mate, chosen as one who would appreciate "the good life" and share it with me. And from the very beginning it had been nothing but hell—hell and torment. To make it worse, the neighbors regarded her as a model creature—so spry, so lively, so generous, so warm. Such a good little mother, such an excellent housewife, such a perfect hostess! It's not easy to live with a man thirty years older, a writer to boot, and especially a writer like Henry Miller. Everyone knew that. Everyone could see that she was doing her utmost. She had courage, that girl!

And hadn't I made a failure of it before? Several times, in fact?

81

Could any woman on earth possibly get along with a man like me? That's how most of our arguments ended, on that note. What to answer? There was no answer. Convicted, sentenced, condemned to rehearse the situation over and over, until one or the other should fall apart, dissolve like a rotting corpse.

Not a day of peace, not a day of happiness, unless on my own. The moment she opened her mouth—war!

It sounds so simple: break it up! get a divorce! separate! But what about the child? Where would I stand, in court, claiming the right to keep my daughter? "You? A man with your reputation?" I could just see the judge foaming at the mouth.

Even to do away with myself would not remedy matters. We had to go on. We had to fight it out. No, that's not the word. Iron things out. (With what? A flatiron?) Compromise! That's better. It's not either! Then surrender! Admit you're licked. Let her walk over you. Pretend you don't feel, don't hear, don't see. Pretend you're dead.

Or—get yourself to believe that all is good, all is God, that there is nothing but good, nothing but God who is all goodness, all light, all love. Get yourself to believe. . . . Impossible! One has to just believe. Punkt! Nor is that enough. You have to know. More than that. . . . You have to know that you know.

And what if, despite everything, you find her standing before you, mocking, jeering, deriding, denigrating, sneering, lying, falsifying, distorting, belittling, calling black white, smiling disdainfully, hissing like a snake, nagging, backbiting, shooting out quills like a porcupine. . .? What then?

Why, you say it's God manifesting, it's love appearing

—only in reverse.

And then?

You look through the negative . . . until you see the positive.

Try it sometime—as a morning exercise. Preferably after standing on your head for five minutes. If it doesn't work, get down on your knees and pray.

82

It *will* work, it's got to work!

That's where you're wrong. If you think it's got to, it won't.

But it must, eventually. Otherwise you'll scratch yourself to death.

What is it my friend Alan Watts says? "When it is clear beyond all doubt that the itch cannot be scratched, it stops itching by itself."

On the way home I stopped at the edge of the clearing, where the huge abandoned horse trough stood, to see if the pots and pans were in order. Tomorrow, the weather permitting, little Val would fix me another make-believe breakfast. And I would probably give her a few make-believe suggestions for improving the bacon and eggs, or the oatmeal, or whatever she might decide to serve me. *Make believe. . . .* Make believe you're happy. Make believe you're free. Make believe you're God. Make believe it's all Mind.

I thought of Moricand. "I'll get down on my knees and pray, if that's what she wants." How idiotic! He might equally well have said: "I'll dance, I'll sing, I'll whistle, I'll stand on my head . . . if that's what she wants," *She* wants. As if she wanted anything but his welfare.

I got to thinking of the Zen masters, one old dog in particular. The one who said, "It's your mind that's troubling you, is it? Well then, bring it out, put it down here, let's have a look at it!" Or words to that effect.

I wondered how long the poor devil would continue scratching himself if every time he dug his nails into his flesh one of those gay old dogs would appear out of the ether and give him thirty-nine blows with a stout cudgel.

And yet you know that when you get home she'll be facing you and you'll lose your temper!

Scratch that!

She need only say: "I thought you were in your studio working."

And you'll say: "Must I work all the time? Can't I take a walk once in a while?"

And like that, the fur will fly, and you won't be able to see

83

through the negative. . . . You'll see red, then black, then green, then purple.

Such a beautiful day! Did *you* make it? Did *she* make it? Fuck who made it! Let's go down and see what she wants to fight about. God made it, that's who.

So I go down, bristling like a porcupine.

Fortunately, Jean Wharton's there. Moricand's already been to see her. And she's given her consent.

How different the atmosphere is when Jean's around! As if the sun were pouring through all the windows with intensified light and warmth and love. At once I feel normal. Like my real self. One couldn't possibly bicker and wrangle with a person like Jean Wharton. At least, *I* couldn't. I take a look at my wife. Does she look any different? To be honest, she does. For one thing, there's no fight in her now. She too looks normal. Like any other human being, I'd say.

I won't go so far as to say that I can see God in her. No.

Anyway, there's a lull.

"So you're going to take him on?" I say.

"Yes," says Jean, "he seems to be desperately in earnest. Of course, it won't be easy."

I was going to say, "What language will you talk?" but the question answered itself. God's language, of course!

With anyone else it was bound to work. With Moricand. . . ?

God can talk to a stone wall and make it respond. But the human mind can be thicker, harder to penetrate, than even a wall of steel. What is it the Hindus say? "If God wished to hide, **He** would choose man to hide in."

That evening, as I was going up the garden steps to have a last look around, I met Jean sailing through the gate. She had a lantern in one hand and what seemed like a book in the other. She seemed to be floating through the air. Her feet were on the ground all right, but her body had no weight. She looked more beautiful, more radiant, than I had ever seen her before. Truly an emissary

84

of light and love, of peace and serenity. In the few years since I first met her, at the Big Sur Post Office, she had gone through a definite transformation. Whatever she believed in, whatever it was that she was practicing, it had altered her physically as well as mentally and spiritually. Had I been Moricand, at that moment, I would have been made whole instantly.

But it didn't work out that way. It didn't work at all, as a matter of fact. A fiasco from start to finish.

It was the next morning that I got a full report from Moricand. He was not only incensed, he was outraged. "Such nonsense!" he cried. "Am I a child, a fool, an idiot, that I should be treated thus?"

I let him rave. After he had calmed down I got the details, at least the important one to his way of thinking. The fly in the ointment, what was it but *Science and Health!* He had done his best, he said, to follow Jean Wharton's talk—apparently he had understood almost nothing. The talk was difficult enough to swallow but then, in taking leave, she had thrust this Mary Baker Eddy book under his nose, urging him to read a few passages and dwell on them. She had indicated the passages she thought best to concentrate on. To Moricand, of course, the *Key to the Scriptures* had about as much value as a child's primer. Less, indeed. He had spent his whole life denying, ridiculing, suppressing this kind of "nonsense." What he had expected of Jean Wharton was a laying on of hands, a magical rapport which would aid him in exorcising the demon that made him scratch night and day. The last thing on earth he wanted was a spiritual interpretation of the art of healing. Or shall I say what is nearer the truth—that he did not want to be told he could heal himself, that indeed he *must* heal himself!

When I met Jean, a little later, and related what he had told me, she explained that she had left the book with him, not with any intention of converting him to Christian Science, but simply to make him forget himself for a while. She had understood him,

85

his French, clearly enough and she had been prepared to wrestle with him anew the next night and for as many nights as might be necessary. She confessed that perhaps it had been a mistake to give him Mary Baker Eddy to read. However, as she well said, had he been sincere, had he been willing to surrender just the least bit, he would not have been so outraged by the book. A man who is desperate can find comfort in anything, sometimes even in that which goes against the grain.

The discussion about the book incited me to have a look at it myself. I had read quite a little about Mary Baker Eddy but I had never, strangely enough, gone to the book itself. I discovered immediately that I was in for a pleasant surprise. Mary Baker Eddy became very real to me. My critical opinion of her fell away. I saw her as the great soul she was, human, yes, human to the core, but filled with a great light, transformed by a revelation such as might occur to any of us were we big enough and open enough to receive it.

As for Moricand, it was as if we had removed the last stepping stone from under his feet. He was depressed as never before. Absolutely despondent, wretched, miserable. Every night he wailed like a banshee. Instead of an *apéritif* before dinner he would treat us to an exhibition of his sores. "It's inhuman," he would say. "You've got to *do* something!" Then, with a sigh, "If only I could take a warm bath!"

We had no bath tub. We had no miracle drugs. We had nothing but words, empty words. At any rate, by now he was just a flaming wretch who had delivered himself to the mercy of the Devil.

Only one evening before the final breakdown stands out clearly. I remember it well because earlier that evening, while we were still eating, he had expressed his irritation with Val, who was sitting beside him, in a way I can never forget. Bored with the conversation, she had begun to play with the knives and forks, rattle the dishes, anything to gain attention. Suddenly, in a playful way, she had snatched the piece of bread lying beside him. Furious, he snatched it from her fist and placed it on the other side of his plate. It was not the gesture of annoyance so much as the look in his eyes which startled me. It was a look full of hatred, the look of a man so beside himself that he might even commit murder. I never forgot it and I never forgave it.

It was a hour or two later, after the child had been put to bed, that he launched into a lengthy tale which I shall recapitulate briefly. What provoked it I no longer remember. But it was about a child, a girl of eight or nine. The telling of it seemed to take up the entire evening.

As often happened, when beginning a yarn, he shrouded the opening in irrelevant wrappings. It was not until (following him down the *grands boulevards*) he made mention of the Passage Jouffroy that I was aware that he was spinning a tale. The Passage Jouffroy happens to be one of those arcades which are freighted with souvenirs for me. Many thing had happened to me, in years gone by, while strolling through that well-known landmark. I mean inner happenings, events one never thinks to write about because too fleeting, too impalpable, too close to the source.

And now here is Moricand suddenly shocking me into awareness of the fact that he is following on the heels of a woman and her daughter. They have just turned into the Passage Jouffroy, window shopping, seemingly. *When* he began following them, *why, how long,* has lost importance. It's the sudden inner excitement which his looks and gestures betray that takes hold of me, rivets my attention.

I thought at first it was the mother he was interested in. He had described her swiftly, deftly, much as a painter would. Described her as only Moricand could describe a woman of that type. In a few words he had stripped her of her nondescript garb, her pseudo-maternal air, her pretense of strolling the boulevards with her in-nocent little lamb. He had recognized her for what she was the moment she had turned into the Passage Jouffroy, that moment

87

when she had hesitated just the fraction of a second, as if she were about to look back, but didn't. He knew then that *she* knew he was following.

It was almost painful to hear him rhapsodize about the little girl. What was it about her that so excited him? *The look of the perverted angel!*

His words were so graphic, so diabolically searching, that despite myself, I was ready to believe that the child was steeped in vice. *Or else so innocent that. . . .*

The thought of what was passing through his mind made me shudder.

What followed was mere routine. *He* took a stand before a window display of manikins dressed in latest sports models while a few feet away the woman and child dallied to gaze upon a virginal figure garbed in a beautiful Communion dress. Observing that the child was rapt in wonder, he threw the woman a quick glance and nodded meaningfully toward her charge. The woman responded with the barest perceptible sway of her head, lowered her eyes a moment, then, looking straight at him, through him, grasped the child's hand and led her away. He permitted them to get a respectable distance ahead, then followed in their wake. Near the exit the woman stopped a moment to turn her bowed head in the direction of his feet; she then resumed what was to all appearances an innocent promenade. Once or twice the little girl made as if to turn around, as would any child whose attention had been caught by the flutter of pigeon wings or the gleam of glass beads.

There was no increase in their pace. The mother and daughter sauntered along as if taking the air, enjoying the sights. Leisurely they turned down one street and up another. Gradually they approached the neighborhood of the Folies-Bergère. Finally they came to a hotel, a hotel with a rather flamboyant name. (I mention it because I recognized the name; I had spent a week in this hotel once, in bed most of the time. During that week, flat on my back, I had read Céline's *Voyage au bout de la nuit*.)

88

Even as they entered the woman made no visible effort to see if he were following. She had no need to look: it had all been worked out telepathically in the Passage Jouffroy.

He waited outside a few moments to collect himself, then, though his guts were still quivering, he walked calmly up to the desk and booked a room. As he filled out the *fiche* the woman laid her key down a moment to stuff something in her purse. He didn't even have to turn his head to catch the number. He gave the *garçon* a liberal tip and, since he had no bags, told him it was unnecessary to show him the way. By the time he reached the top of the first flight of stairs his heart was in his mouth. He bounded up the next flight, turned quickly down the passage towards the room he was looking for, and came face to face with the woman. Though there was not a soul about, neither paused an instant. They brushed by each other like two strangers, she as if going to the lavatory, he as if to his room. Only the look in her eyes, the drooping, sidewise glance, conveyed the message he knew was forthcoming: *"Elle est là!"* He walked swiftly to the door, removed the key which had been left outside, and pushed his way in.

Here he paused in his narration. His eyes were positively dancing. I knew he was waiting for me to say "Then what?" I struggled with myself not to reveal my true feelings. The words he was waiting for got stuck in my throat. All I could think of was the little girl sitting on the edge of the bed, half-undressed probably, and nibbling at a piece of pastry. *"Reste-là, p'tite, je reviens toute de suite,"* the woman had probably said as she closed the door behind her.

Finally, after what seemed like an eternity, I heard myself saying to him: *"Eh bien,* what then?"

"What then?" he exclaimed, his eyes aflame with a ghoulish glee. *"Je l'ai eue,* that's what!"

As he uttered these words I felt my hair stand on end. It was no longer Moricand I was facing but Satan himself.

89

The rains continued to descend, the leaks grew worse, the walls got wetter and wetter, the sow bugs increased and multiplied. The horizon was now completely shut out; the wind had become a howling fury. Back of the two studios stood three tall eucalyptus trees; under the lash of the gale they seemed to bend in two. In Moricand's shattered state they were three demons with a thousand arms beating a terrifying tattoo upon his brainpan. Wherever he looked, indeed, there was nothing but a wall of water, a forest of swaying, swirling, twisting tree trunks. And with it, what disturbed him more than anything, the whine and moan of the wind, the whistling, crackling, hissing sound which never abated. To anyone in his right senses it was grand, magnificent, absolutely intoxicating. One felt deliciously helpless, insignificant, even less than a rubber doll. To venture outdoors at the height of it was to be slapped down. There was something insane about it. All you could do was to wait it out. It must die of its own fury.

But Moricand could not wait it out. He was at the breaking point. He came down one afternoon—it was already dark—saying that he couldn't stand it another minute. "It's a howling inferno!" he cried. "Nowhere in the world can it possibly rain like this. *C'est fou!*"

At dinner, rehearsing his miseries, he suddenly burst into tears. He begged me—supplicated, rather—to do something to relieve him of his torment. He pleaded and entreated as if I were made of stone. It was sheer torture to listen to the man.

"What *can* I do?" said I. "What is it you think I *should* do?"

"Take me to Monterey. Put me in a hospital. I *must* get out of this place."

"Very well," I said. "I'll do that. I'll move you just as soon as we can get off this hill."

What did that mean? he wanted to know. A feeble look of terror spread over his countenance.

I explained that not only was my car not working but that the road leading to the highway was blocked with boulders; the storm would have to abate before we could even think about moving.

90

This only increased his desperation. *"Think, think!"* he begged. "There must be some way to get out of here. Do you want me to go stark mad?"

The only thing left to do was to walk down the road to the highway next morning and leave a note in the mailbox for the mail man to deliver to Lilik. The mail was still getting through. All day long and into the night the highway crew kept clearing the road of debris. I knew that Lilik would get to us if it were humanly possible. As for the boulders that blocked the foot of the road, I would just pray that some Titan would push them aside.

So I got down, dispatched the message, making it life and death, and told Moricand to be in readiness. I had told Lilik to come the next morning, at six o'clock, or perhaps I said five-thirty. I figured that by that time the storm would have moderated and some of the boulders been cleared away.

That night, his last night, Moricand refused to go back to his cell. He decided to sit up all night in the armchair. We kept him at table as long as we could, plied him with drink, regaled him as best we could, and finally, towards morning, bade him goodnight. There was just the one room, and our bed was in the middle of it. We climbed in and tried to go to sleep. A tiny lamp flickered on the table beside him as he sat in the big armchair, bundled up in overcoat and muffler, his hat pulled down over his eyes. The fire went out, and though not a window was open, the room soon grew damp and chill. The wind was still whistling around the corners of the house, but it seemed to me that the rain was letting up.

Naturally, I couldn't sleep. I lay there as quiet as I could and listened to him mumbling to himself. Every now and then he groaned and broke out with a *"Mon Dieu, mon Dieu!* when will it end?" Or—*"Quel supplice!"*

About 5:00 A.M. I climbed out of bed, lit the Aladdin lamps, put some coffee on the stove, and dressed. It was still dark, but the storm had broken. There was just a normal high wind which was sweeping away the rain.

When I asked him how he felt, he groaned. Never had he

91

known such a night. He was finished. He hoped he would have the strength to last till we reached the hospital.

As we were swallowing the hot coffee, he got a whiff of the bacon and eggs. That gave him a momentary lift. *"J'adore ça,"* he said, rubbing his hands. Then a sudden panic seized him. "How do we know he will come, Lilik?"

"He'll come, never fear," I said. "He would wade through Hell to rescue you."

"Oui, c'est un chic type. Un vrai ami."

By this time my wife had dressed, set the table, lit the stove, served the bacon and eggs.

"Everything will be fine," she said. "You'll see, Lilik will be here in a few minutes." She spoke to him as if he were a child. (Don't worry, dear, mamma's here, nothing can happen to you.)

Seized with a sense of the dramatic, I suddenly decided to light the lantern and go to the top of the road above us to signal Lilik. As I climbed the hill I heard his car snorting down below, probably at the bend near the Roosevelt's. I waved the lantern to and fro and, now thoroughly elated, gave a great shout. He must have seen the light, for immediately there came the honk-honk of his horn, and in a few moments the car came into sight, puffing and snorting like a wounded dragon.

"Christ!" I shouted, "What luck! You made it! *Grand!*" I gave him a warm hug.

"I had a bad time of it down below," he said. "I don't know how I ever cleared those rocks away. Luckily, I brought a crowbar with me. . . . How's Moricand? Is he awake yet?"

"Is he awake? Man, he's never been to sleep. Come on down and have a cup of coffee. Have you had breakfast?"

He hadn't. Not even a cup of coffee.

We walked in, and there was Moricand licking his chops. He seemed quite revived. As he greeted Lilik, tears came to his eyes. *"C'est la fin,"* he said. "But how good of you to come! You're a saint."

When it came time to go Moricand rose to his feet, tottered, staggered to the bed and collapsed.

"What's up?" cried Lilik. "You're not going to give out now, are you?"

Moricand looked up woefully. "I can't walk," he said. "Look!" And he pointed to the swelling between his legs.

"What's that?" we cried in unison.

"My testicles!" he exclaimed. "They've swollen up on me." They had indeed. They were like two rocks.

"We'll carry you to the car," said Lilik.

"I'm too heavy," said Moricand.

"Nonsense!" said Lilik.

Moricand put his arms around our shoulders, and Lilik and I joined hands under his legs. He weighed a ton. Slowly, gently, we hoisted him up the garden steps and into the car. He groaned like a bull in agony.

"Easy, easy now. It will pass. Just hold your breath, grit your teeth. Du courage, mon vieux!"

As we cautiously picked our way down the winding hill, observing the havoc the storm had wrought, Moricand's eyes opened wider and wider. Finally we came to the last stretch, a rather steep descent. Huge boulders towered above menacingly. When we reached the highway I saw what Lilik had done. It didn't seem possible for human hands to have accomplished such a task.

Dawn had come, the rain had stopped altogether, and we were on our way. Every few yards we had to stop and clear the road of debris. This continued until we reached the sign which said: "Watch for falling rocks. Dangerous curves and falling rocks for the next 46 miles." But that was all behind us now.

My thoughts reverted to Moricand's promenade between the battlefronts. The two valises. And Iamblichus! By comparison, all that seemed unreal, a nightmare that he had dreamed up.

"How do your balls feel now?" I asked.

He felt them. Somewhat better, he thought.

"Good," said Lilik. "It's just nervousness."

I restrained a laugh. "Nervousness! What a word to describe Moricand's anguish!

When we got to Monterey we stopped to fetch him a cup of coffee. The sun was out strong, the roof-tops glistened; life was pursuing its normal course again. Only a few more miles, we told him, and you'll be there. Meaning at the County Hospital in Salinas.

He felt his testicles again. The swelling had almost disappeared.

"What did we tell you!"

"Ouais!" said Moricand. *"Mais, c'est drôle.* How do you explain it?"

"Nervousness," said Lilik.

"Angoisse!" said I.

We rolled up in front of the hospital. It didn't look as bad as I had imagined it would. From the outside, in fact, it seemed rather cheerful. Just the same, I was glad it wasn't my turn.

We went inside. It was still rather early. The usual routine: questions, explanations, papers to fill out. Then wait. No matter if you're dying, they always ask you to wait.

We waited a while, then inquired when the doctor would show up. I had thought we would get Moricand a bed immediately, then see the doctor. No, first you see the doctor, then a bed—if there is one vacant!

We decided to have a second breakfast. There was a glassed-in dining room which was connected with the hospital, or so it seemed to me. We had bacon and eggs again. And more coffee. The coffee was vile and weak, but Moricand said it tasted good. He lit a *gauloise bleue*—and smiled. He was probably thinking of the comfortable bed, the attention he would receive, the luxury of relaxing in the midst of ministering angels.

Finally it came time to visit the clinic. It was like all such places, cold, bare, glittering with instruments, smelling of dis-

94

infectants. You bring your poor, frail body and you hand it over to be inspected. You are one thing and your body is another. Lucky you if you get it back again.

He's standing there nude, naked as a herring. The doctor is tapping at him, just like a woodpecker. We've explained that it's the itch he's suffering from. No matter. Must see if there's anything else first—phthisis, gallstones, asthma, tonsilitis, cirrhosis of the liver, miner's elbow, dandruff. . . . The doctor's not a bad chap. Affable, courteous, willing to chatter. Speaks French too. Rather pleased on the whole to see a specimen like Moricand for a change.

Moricand too seems rather pleased. At last some real attention. Something indefinable about his expression gives me the impression that he hopes the doctor will find something seriously wrong with him, something more than the itch.

Without a stitch he looks lamentable. Like a broken-down nag. It's not merely that he's potbellied, full of sores and scabs, but that his skin has an unhealthy look, is spotted like tobacco leaf, has no oil, no elasticity, no glow. He looks like one of those derelicts one sees in the washroom of a Mills hotel, like a bum that has just crawled out of a flophouse on the Bowery. His flesh seems never to have been in contact with air and sun; it looks half-smoked.

The physical examination over, and nothing seriously wrong except that he's run-down, anemic, bilious, weak heart, erratic pulse, high blood pressure, spavined and double-jointed, it's now time to investigate the itch.

It's the doctor's opinion that he's suffering from an allergy, perhaps several allergies. Allergies are his specialty. Hence his certitude.

No one demurs, not even Moricand. He's heard of allergies but never attached any importance to them. Neither have I. Neither has Lilik. However, today it's allergies. Tomorrow it will be something else. Allergies then. Go to it!

95

While assorting and arranging his test tubes, syringes, needles, razor blades and what not, in preparation for the tests, the doctor plies Moricand with questions.

"You've had the drug habit, haven't you?"

Moricand nods.

"I can tell," says the doctor, pointing to Moricand's legs, arms, thighs, where traces of the needle still showed.

"What did you use?"

"Everything," said Moricand. "But that was some years ago."

"Opium too?"

At this Moricand seemed somewhat surprised. "How did you know?" he asked.

"I've treated thousands of cases," said the doctor. He fiddled with something behind Moricand's back. As he wheeled around, he said swiftly: "How did you break it, tell me that!"

"By my own will," said Moricand.

"What's that?" said the doctor. "Say it again!"

Moricand repeated: "By my own will. It was not easy. It almost killed me."

"If that's true," said the doctor, taking his hand, "you're the first man I've known to accomplish it."

Moricand blushed as a man might who was being given a medal for a deed of valor he had never performed.

Meanwhile the doctor had begun the game of ticktacktoe on Moricand's back. He started up near the left shoulder, worked clear across to the right shoulder, then down and across. Each time he finished a game he waited a few minutes. The first game was all in blue ink, the second in pink, the third in green, and so on through the spectrum. Nobody was winning. Since Moricand's back was only human size, and since it was completely covered with welts from neck to waist, there was nothing to do but call it a draw for the day. There were still thirty or forty more tests that could be given. One of them had to turn out positive. At least, that was how the doctor regarded it.

96

"And now what about a bed?" said Moricand, slipping into his shirt and trousers.

"A *bed?*" said the doctor, looking at him in astonishment.

"Yes," said Moricand. "A place to rest . . . to recuperate."

The doctor laughed as if it were a good joke.

"We don't have beds enough for our serious cases," he said. "There's nothing very wrong with you. Come back day after tomorrow and I'll give you some more tests." He wrote out a prescription for a sedative. "You'll be all right in no time."

I explained that we lived in Big Sur, that it wasn't easy to make frequent trips to Salinas.

"Why don't you put him up in town for a while?" said the doctor. "In a week or so I'll know what's what. There's nothing to worry about. He's been through much worse, I can tell you that. . . . Just a bit dilapidated. Hypersensitive."

Outside we decided to look for a bar. We all needed a drink bad.

"How does your back feel?" said Lilik, raising his hands as if to give him a clap.

Moricand winced. "It feels like a hot grill," he said.

We found a dingy bar and, while putting away a few drinks, discussed the opium habit. An illuminating subject, if one penetrates deeply enough.

In Monterey I engaged a room for him at the Hotel Serra. A room with a private bath. In comparison with the cell he had been living in this was luxury. We tested the bed to see if it was soft and springy enough, switched the lights on and off to see if they were good enough to read and write by, showed him how to manipulate the window blinds, assured him that he would get fresh towels and soap every day, and so on. He was already unpacking the small valise he had brought along. Already the dresser was arranged as he invariably arranged things wherever he might find himself. As he was getting out his manuscripts, his writing tablet, his ink and ruler, I suddenly realized that the table beside the bed would be too small to work on. We called the manager to

97

find if he couldn't supply a bigger one. In a jiffy the bellhop arrived with a table just the right size.

Moricand seemed really overcome with joy. He looked around as if he were in Heaven. The bathroom especially put him in ecstasy. We had explained that he could take a bath as often as he wished—no extra charge, as in France. (This was the good side of America again. "A wonderful country!")

It only remained now to hand him some money and arrange with someone who had a car to drive him back and forth to the hospital. I didn't know, as I said *au revoir*, that it would be the last time I would see him.

He had grown ten years younger in the space of a few minutes. As we shook hands, as I promised to look him up in a few days, he said: "I think I'll go down in a little while to have a *porto*."

Walking down the street, Lilik and I, we ran into the painter, Ellwood Graham. After a few words we learned that he was making trips to the County Hospital every day. It would be a pleasure he informed us, to drive Moricand back and forth.

We ducked back to the hotel immediately only to find that Moricand had already left, presumably to have his *porto*. We left a note explaining that he would have the use of a car and a private chauffeur.

The feeling of relief I experienced on arriving home was beyond words. It was high time we were rid of him, for my wife was already pregnant several months. Yet she had borne up under the ordeal better than I.

A few days passed but I simply could not bring myself to go to Monterey and look him up. Instead I wrote him a note, making some excuse or other. He wrote back immediately to say that he was feeling better, that the doctor hadn't discovered yet what was wrong with him, but that he was enjoying his most comfortable quarters. A postscript reminded me that the rent would be due in a few days, also that he would need some fresh linen soon.

We exchanged notes for about two weeks or so, during which time I did go to town but without looking him up. Then one day I received word that he had made up his mind to go to San Francisco; he thought he could find something to do there, and, if not, he would make efforts to return to Paris. He added that it was obvious I didn't wish to see him any more.

On receipt of this message I immediately packed the remainder of his belongings, had someone deliver them to him at the hotel, and sent him enough money to last him a couple of weeks at least. That he was putting this much distance between us gave me a still greater feeling of relief. And the fact that he had at last found enough gumption to do something on his own.

I then fumigated his cell, as Leon had recommended.

In writing him I had given him elaborate explanations and instructions. I told him where to look for modest French restaurants, bars, and so forth. I even went to the extent of telling him that if he could not make himself understood he was to write the address down and show it to the cab-driver, the policeman, or whoever it might be. I told him where to find the library, the avant-garde cinemas, the museums and art galleries.

I soon learned that he had found a suitable hotel, but at a much higher rate than I had named; he had also discovered a little bar where he could get his meals and where there were a few congenial French people. His money was going fast, he explained, because wherever he wanted to go he had to take a cab; he wouldn't trust himself to take streetcars and buses, his English was too poor.

To all this I gave a patient ear, thinking that he would soon adjust himself and settle down to a less expensive routine. The business about the cabs nettled me. Paris was a far bigger city than San Francisco and I had managed to find my way about in it with less money in my jeans and less knowledge of French than he had of English. But then I had no one to fall back on. *Ça fait une différence!*

He had, of course, reported to the Swiss Consul and had quickly learned that there was no question of finding employment, not with a visitor's visa. He could, to be sure, take steps to become an American citizen, but he was not interested in becoming an American citizen.

What *was* he going to do, I wondered? Would he request the Swiss Consul to ship him back to Paris?

Perhaps he had asked the Swiss Consul to ship him home and perhaps they had told him that that was *my* responsibility. At any rate, the impression I got was that he was simply drifting with the tide. As long as I could keep him in food, cigarettes, taxi fares, a comfortable room and bath, he was not going to get panicky. San Francisco suited him far better than Big Sur, even though he found it somewhat "provincial." At least there was solid pavement under his feet.

It was after he had been there over a month that the effort to maintain him in his own style became a strain. I had the feeling that the arrangement could continue indefinitely, so far as *he* was concerned. Finally I suggested that if he were seriously of a mind to return to Europe I would see what I could do to get him a passage back. Instead of being elated he replied in gloomy vein that if it came to a pinch, why yes, he would go back. As if he were doing me a great favor to even consider the thought!

It so happened that shortly after this exchange of views my good friend, Raoul Bertrand, came to visit us. He had met Moricand at our home several times and knew what I was up against. When I explained how matters now stood he volunteered to see if he could not secure passage for Moricand on a French freighter plying from San Francisco. A free passage, moreover.

I immediately apprised Moricand of the good news and drew an alluring picture of a long sea voyage through the Panama Canal, with stopovers in Mexico and Central America. I made it sound so enchanting that I began to wish I could change places with him. What his reply was precisely, I no longer recall, only that he gave a grudging acquiescence. Meanwhile Bertrand had set to work. In

100

less than a week he had found a freighter which offered Moricand passage. It would leave in thirty-six hours—just time enough to send Moricand a wire. In order to circumvent any misinterpretation of the message on the part of the telegraph company, I wrote the message out in English: a fifty-word telegram giving full details.

To my utter astonishment, I got a reply by mail after the boat had sailed, saying that his Highness was not to be rushed that way, that he should have had a few days' warning at least, that it was most inconsiderate of me to send him a message of such importance in a language he didn't understand, and so on and so forth. Extremely hoity-toity, to put it mildly. Besides, as he went on to explain in a postscript, he was not at all certain that he would relish a long sea voyage; he was not a good sailor, he would be bored to death, etc., etc. At the very end—would I please send him some more money!

I was thoroughly incensed. And I let him know it in no uncertain terms. Then I wrote a profuse letter of apology to Raoul Bertrand. Here he was, a French consul, not Swiss, putting himself to all this trouble, and that louse, Moricand, hadn't even the decency to be grateful for his efforts.

Bertrand, however, understood better than I the manner of man we were dealing with. He was not at all perturbed or dismayed. "We'll try again," he said. "You've got to get him off your hands!" He added: "Perhaps next time we'll get him a plane passage. He can hardly refuse that."

And by God, in about ten days he did come up with a plane passage. This time we gave Moricand ample notice.

Once again he agreed, grumblingly, to be sure. Like a rat that had been cornered. But when the time came to depart he was not on hand. He had changed his mind again. What excuse he gave I no longer remember.

By this time a number of my intimate friends had got wind of "the Moricand affair," as they called it. Everywhere I went people would ask—"What's happened to your friend? Did you get rid of him yet? Has he had the courage to let me know in plain language that I was nothing but an idiot. "Cut him loose, Henry, or you'll never get him off your hands! He'll bleed you dry." That was the general tenor of the advice I received.

One day Varda came to see me. He was now living in Sausalito on a ferry boat which he had converted into a houseboat, dance palace and studio. He was all agog about the Moricand business, having received all the juicy details from a dozen different sources. His attitude was one of high amusement and genuine concern. How could he get in touch with Moricand? He referred to him as some sort of parasitic monster for whom saints and simpletons were easy prey.

Regarding me as an utterly helpless victim, he then proposed a typical Varda solution. He said he knew a wealthy woman in San Francisco, a Hungarian or Austrian countess, still attractive though aging, who loved to "collect" bizarre figures such as Moricand. Astrology, occultism—that was just her meat. She had a huge mansion, money to burn, and thought nothing of having a guest remain a year or two. If Moricand were as good a talker as I said he was, he would be an attraction for her salon. Celebrities from all over the world converged there, he said. It would be a real haven for a man like Moricand.

"I'll tell you what I'll do," he went on. "As soon as I get back to Sausalito I'll ask her to arrange a soirée. I'll see that Moricand is invited. The man has only to open his mouth and she'll be hooked."

"Are you sure she won't expect something more of him?" said I. "An aging countess, and still attractive, as you say, may make demands Moricand is no longer able to satisfy."

"Don't worry about *that!*" he cried, giving me a knowing look. "She has only to wave her hand and she can have the pick of San Francisco's finest young blades. Besides, she has a pair of the

102

most lecherous-looking lap dogs you ever laid eyes on. No, if she takes him, she'll use him for her salon."

I regarded Varda's proposal as a huge joke. Thought no more of it, indeed. Meantime another letter arrived from Moricand, a letter full of recriminations. Why was I in such haste to pack him off? What had he ever done to deserve such treatment? Was it his fault that he had fallen ill *chez moi*? He reminded me caustically that I was still responsible for his welfare, that I had signed papers to that effect, and that he had these papers in his possession. He even insinuated that if I didn't toe the mark he would inform the proper authorities of the scandal my books had created in France. (As if they didn't know!) He might even tell them worse things about me . . . that I was an anarchist, a traitor, a renegade, and what all.

I was ready to hit the ceiling. "That bastard!" I said. "He's actually beginning to threaten me."

Meanwhile Bertrand was making efforts to get him a second plane passage. And Lilik was getting ready to go to Berkeley on a business errand. He too was going to do something about this damned Moricand business. At least he would see him and try to talk some sense into him.

Then came a letter from Varda. He had arranged a soiree *chez* the Countess, had primed her for the jewel she was to get, found her sympathetic to the idea, and. . . . To make it short, Moricand had come, had taken one look at the Countess, and then had avoided her like sin for the rest of the evening. He had remained silent and glum the whole evening, except to unleash a cutting remark now and then about the vanity and stupidity of wealthy émigrées who exploited their salons to rustle up fresh bait to whet their jaded appetites.

"The bastard!" I said to myself. "Couldn't even take on a millionairess to help a fellow out!"

On the heels of this incident Bertrand came up with another plane passage, this one a good week off. Once again I informed

103

his Highness that a silver bird of the air was at his disposal. Would he be so gracious as to give it a trial?

This time the response was clear and definite. All mystery was ripped away.

I give the gist of his letter. . . . Yes, he would consent to accept the passage which had been proffered him, but on one condition, that I first put to his account in a Paris bank the equivalent of a thousand dollars. It should be easy to understand the reason for such a request. He had left Europe as a pauper and he had no intention of returning as one. It was I who had induced him to come to America, and I had promised to take care of him. It was not his wish to return to Paris, but mine. I wanted to get rid of him, renounce my sacred obligation. As for the money I had spent thus far—he referred to it as if it were a bagatelle—he begged to remind me that he had left with me as a gift an heirloom, his one and only material possession, which was priceless. (He meant the *pendule*, of course.)

I was outraged. I wrote back at once that if he didn't take the plane this time, if he didn't get the hell out of the country and leave me in peace, I would cut him off. I said I didn't give a shit what became of him. He could jump off the Golden Gate Bridge, for all I cared. In a postscript I informed him that Lilik would be there to see him in a day or two, *with the pendule*, which he could shove up his ass, or pawn and live on the proceeds for the rest of his days.

Now the letters came thick and fast. He was in a panic. Cut him off? Leave him destitute? Alone in a foreign land? A man who was ill, who was getting old, who had no right to seek employment? No, I would never do that! Not the Miller he had known of old, the Miller with a great, compassionate heart who gave to one and all, who had taken pity on him, a miserable wretch, and sworn to provide for him as long as he lived!

"Yes," I wrote back, "it is the same Miller. He is fed up. He is disgusted. He wants nothing more to do with you." I called him a worm, a leech, a dirty blackmailer.

He turned to my wife. Long, whining letters, full of self-pity. Surely *she* understood his plight! The good Miller had taken leave of his senses, he had made himself into stone. *Le pauvre*, he would regret it some day. And so on and so on.

I urged my wife to ignore his pleas. I doubt that she heeded me. She felt sorry for him. It was her belief that he would come to his senses at the last minute, take the plane, forget his foolish demand. "Foolish!" she called it.

I thought of Ramakrishna's words regarding the "bound" souls. "Those who are thus caught in the net of the world are the *Baddha*, or bound souls. No one can awaken them. They do not come to their senses, even after receiving blow upon blow of misery, sorrow and indescribable suffering,"

I thought of many, many things during the hectic days which followed. Particularly of the beggar's life I had led, first at home, then abroad. I thought of the cold refusals I had received at the hands of intimate friends, of so-called "buddies," in fact. I thought of the meals which were dished up to me, when I hung on like a shipwrecked sailor. And the sermons that accompanied them. I thought of the times I had stood in front of restaurant windows, watching people eat—people who didn't need food, who had already eaten too much—and how I vainly hoped they would recognize the look in my eye, invite me in, beg me to share their repast, or offer me the remnants. I thought of the handouts I had received, the dimes that were flung at me in passing, or perhaps a handful of pennies, and how like a whipped cur, I had taken what was offered while cursing the bastards under my breath. No matter how many refusals I received, and they were countless, no matter how many insults and humiliations were flung at me, a crust of bread was always a crust of bread—and if I didn't always thank the giver graciously or humbly, I did thank my lucky star. I may have thought once upon a time that something more than a crust of bread was my due, that the most worthless wretch, at least in a civilized country, was entitled to a meal when he needed it. But it wasn't long before I learned to take a larger view of things. I

105

not only learned how to say "Thank you, sir!" but how to stand on my hind legs and beg for it. It didn't embitter me hopelessly. In fact, I found it rather comical after a while. It's an experience we all need now and then, especially those of us who were born with silver spoons in our mouths.

But that bastard, Moricand! To twist things the way he did! To make it appear, if only to himself, that in promising to take care of him I was obligated to keep him in a hotel, dole out cash for drink, theatre, taxis. And, if that proved irksome, why just deposit a thousand dollars to his account in Paris. Because he, Moricand, refused to be a pauper again!

I'm on the corner of Broadway and 42nd Street again. A chilly night, and the rain beating in my face. Scanning the throng once again for a friendly face, for a fleeting look that will assure me I won't get a rebuff, won't get a gob of spit instead of a handout. Here's a likely one! "Hey, mister, *please*, can you spare enough for a cup of coffee?" He gives it without stopping, without even looking me in the face. A dime! A lovely, shining little offering. A whole dime! How ducky it would be if one could only catch a generous soul like that on the wing, grab his coattail, pull him gently around, and say with utter conviction and the innocence of a dove: "*Mister*, what can I do with this? I haven't eaten since yesterday morning. I'm cold and wet through. My wife's home waiting for me. She's hungry too. And ill. Couldn't you give me a dollar, or maybe two dollars? *Mister*, we need it bad, terribly bad."

No, it's not in the book, that kind of talk. One has to be grateful even for a Canadian dime—or a stale crust of bread. Grateful that when it comes *your* time to be hooked, you can say—and mean it with all your heart!—"Here, take this! Do what you like with it!" And so saying, empty your pockets. So saying, *you* walk home in the rain, *you* go without a meal!

Have I ever done it? Of course I have. Many's the time. And it felt marvelous to do it. Almost too marvelous. It's easy to

106

empty your pockets when you see your other self standing there like a dog, begging, whimpering, cringing. It's easy to go without a meal when you know you can have one for the asking. Or that tomorrow's another day. Nothing to it. It's you, Prince Bountiful, as gets the better of the deal. No wonder we hang our heads in shame when we perform a simple act of charity.

I wonder sometimes why rich guys never understand this business, why they never take the opportunity to give themselves a cheap puffing up? Think of Henry Miller, the uncrowned emperor of California, coming out of the bank each morning with a pocket filled with quarters, handing them out like King Solomon to the poor blokes lined up the sidewalk, each and every one mumbling humbly, "Thank you, sir!" and raising his hat respectfully. What better tonic could you give yourself, if you had a soul as mean as that, before tackling the day's work?

As for that phony bastard, Moricand, in his palmy days he had been quite a giver too, from all I have heard. Nor had he ever refused to share what he had when he had little or nothing. But he had never gone out into the street and begged for it! When he begged it was on good stationery, in elegant script—grammar, syntax, punctuation always perfect. Never had he sat down to pen a begging letter in trousers that had holes in the seat, or even patches. The room may have been ice cold, his belly may have been empty, the butt in his mouth may have been rescued from the waste basket, but. . . . I think it's clear what I'm getting at.

Anyway, he didn't take the second plane either. And when he wrote, saying that he was putting a curse on me, I didn't doubt for a minute that he meant just what he said. To avoid a repetition, I promptly informed his Satanic majesty that any subsequent letters from him would be left unopened. And with that off my chest, I consigned him to his fate. Never again would he see my handwriting, nor the color of my money.

This didn't stop the flow of letters, to be sure. Letters continued to arrive, *toujours plus espacés*, but they were never opened. They are now in the library at U.C.L.A. Still sealed.

I recall of a sudden the way he worded his break with Cendrars, his old friend of the Foreign Legion days. It was one of those evenings when he had been reviewing the good old days, the wonderful friends he had made—Cendrars, Cocteau, Radiguet, Kisling, Modigliani, Max Jacob, *et alii*—and how one by one they had disappeared, or else deserted him. All but Max. Max had been faithful to the end. But Cendrars, whom he spoke of so warmly, whom he still admired with all his heart—why had Cendrars also deserted him? Here is the way he put it:

"One day—you know how he is!—he got angry with me. And that was the end. I could never reach him again. I tried, but it was useless. The door was shut."

I never revealed to him what Cendrars had said to me one day, in the year 1938, when I made the horrible mistake of telling him that I had become acquainted with his old friend Moricand.

"Moricand?" he said. *"Ce n'est pas un ami. C'est un cadavre vivant."* And the door went shut with a bang.

Well, the *pendule*. I had given it to Lilik to deliver to Moricand. And Lilik had taken it into his head to find out just how valuable the damned thing was. So, before delivering it, he takes it to the very watchmaker whose address Moricand had given me in the event that it should need repair. Its value? According to this bird, who knew something about timepieces, one would be lucky to get fifty dollars for it. An antique dealer might offer a little more. Not much more, however.

"That's ridiculous," I said, when he recounted the incident.

"That's what I thought," said Lilik. "So I took it to an antique dealer, and then to a hock shop. Same story. No market for such junk. They all admired it, of course. Wonderful mechanism. But who wants it?"

"I thought you'd like to know," he added, "since the bugger always made such a fuss about it."

He then went on to tell me of his telephone conversation with Moricand. (Seems the latter was too wrought up to receive him.) It was a conversation that lasted almost a half hour. With Moricand doing all the talking.

"Too bad you weren't there," said Lilik. "He was in top form. I never knew anyone could be so furious, so venomous, and talk so brilliantly at the same time. The things he said about you . . . You know, after the first few minutes I began to enjoy it. Now and then I helped him along, just to see how far he *would* go. Anyway, be on your guard! He's going to do everything in his power to make trouble for you. I really think he's out of his mind. *Cuckoo.* Absolutely. . . . The last thing I remember him saying was that I would read about you in the French papers. He was formulating a *plaidoyer.* Said he would give them, your admirers, the lowdown on their beloved Henry Miller, author of the *Tropics,* sage of the mountain top . . . '*Quel farceur!*' That was his parting shot."

"Didn't he say—'*Je l'aurai*'?"

"Yeah, that's right. He did too."

"I thought as much. *Le couillon!*"

The first intimation I had of Moricand's maneuvers was a letter from the Swiss Consulate in San Francisco. It was a polite, formal letter, informing me of Moricand's visit to their office, his desperate plight, and ended with a desire to have my view of the matter. I replied at some length, offering to send copies of Moricand's letters, and repeating what I had told Moricand, that I was through and that nothing would make me change my mind. To this I received a reply reminding me that, no matter what had taken place, I was, from an official standpoint, Moricand's sponsor. Would I mind sending the letters I had spoken of?

I sent photostat copies of the letters. Then I waited for the next move.

I could well imagine what must have ensued at this point. One couldn't repudiate what was written in one's own hand.

109

The next letter was to the effect that Moricand's was indeed a knotty case, that the poor fellow was obviously not all there. It went on to say that the Consulate would be only too glad to ship him back home had they funds for such a purpose. (They never do, of course.) Perhaps if he, the Vice-Consul, were to come down and talk it over with me, some suitable compromise might be arranged. Meanwhile they would look after Moricand as best they could.

Well, he came, and we had a long talk. Fortunately, my wife was there to corroborate my statements. Finally, after a snack, he brought forth a camera and took some snapshots of us and the surroundings. The place enchanted him. He asked if he could come again, as a friend.

"And that idiot couldn't stand it here!" he said, shaking his head. "Why, it's a Paradise."

"Paradise lost!" I countered.

"What will you do with him?" I ventured to ask, as he was leaving. He shrugged his shoulders.

"What *can* one do?" he said, "with a creature like that?"

Thanking me warmly for all I had done in behalf of a compatriot, expressing his regret for any annoyance he had caused me, he then said: "You must be a man of great patience."

I never had another word from him. Nor did I ever learn what happened to Moricand—until I received a copy of *Le Goéland*, the issue for July-August-September, 1954, announcing the news of his death. It was from the editor of *Le Goéland*, Théophile Briant—Moricand's last and only friend—that I recently received a few facts relating to the interval between our leave-taking in Monterey, hardly three months after his arrival in Big Sur, and his pitiful end.

It was in March 1948 when we parted. How he lasted until the fall of 1949, when he was deported by the immigration authorities, remains a mystery. Not even Briant could tell me much about this period. It was a black one, *évidemment*. Toward the end of September he appeared at Briant's home in Brittany, where he had been offered refuge. Here he lasted only six weks. As Briant

110

tactfully put it in his letter, "I perceived all too quickly that a life in common could not be prolonged indefinitely." Thus, the 17th of November his faithful friend drove him to Paris—and installed him in the same old Hotel Modial. Here, though he held out for some time, things went rapidly from bad to worse. Finally, in utter despair, fate decreed that he should accept the last humiliation, that is, apply for admission to a Swiss retreat for the aged on the Avenue de St. Mandé, Paris. It was an institution founded by his own parents. Here he chose a small cell giving on the courtyard, where from his window he could see the plaque commemorating the inauguration of the establishment by his mother and his brother, Dr. Ivan Moricand.

"*Tous ses amis,*" writes Briant, "*sauf moi, l'avaient abandonné. Ses nombreux manuscrits étaient refoulés chez les éditeurs. Et bien entendu, des drames épais surgirent bientôt entre lui et les directrices de l'Asile. Je m'efforçai de le calmer, lui représentant que cette cellule, qu'il avait d'ailleurs merveilleusement aménagée, constituait son ultime havre de grâce.*"

The end came quite suddenly. According to Briant's obituary article in *Le Goéland,* on the morning of the day he died Moricand received a visit from a dear friend, a woman. This was towards noon. As they parted he informed her quite simply that she would never see him again. As he seemed to be in good health and good spirits, and since nothing in their conversation had warranted such a remark, she dismissed it as a *boutade.* That very afternoon, towards four o'clock, he had a heart attack. He went to the kitchen for aid, but despite his grave condition no one saw any reason for alarm. A doctor was called but he was busy. He would come later, when he was free. When he did arrive it was too late. There was nothing to do but rush poor Moricand, already breathing his last, to the hospital. He was unconscious when they delivered him to the Hospital St. Antoine. At ten-thirty that evening he died without regaining consciousness. August 31st, 1954.

In his last moments, writes Briant, he was "*seul comme un rat, nu comme le dernier des clochards.*"